Love Among the Flames

AMBER HOLLOWAY'S STORY

LOVE IN LEAVENWORTH, WA
BOOK THREE

JUDY LESLIE

According to the National Volunteer Fire Council, of the more than one-million firefighters in the US, 65% of them are volunteers.

I would like to thank all these brave men and women volunteer firefighters that put their lives on the line to help others in their community.

Love Among the Flames

AMBER HOLLOWAY'S STORY

Amber wasn't looking for a fling with an arrogant, rich, city man. She was a woman not afraid to suit up and protect her community.

Mark thought he didn't need anyone until he met the one woman that wasn't impressed by his charm or wealth.

Contents

Chapter One

Amber

I jolt awake, my heart pounding rapidly in my chest as the sound of screaming still echoes in my mind. Gasping for breath, my sheets cling to my skin; I'm damp with sweat. I will my pulse to slow down. *It's not real. It's just a dream.*

As the first light of morning creeps in, the shadows of my nightmare linger in my mind. Easing out of bed, my feet touch the cold floor when I stand up. Slipping into my robe, I wander into the kitchen. Dwelling on my pain will not make the day any easier. Today, my sister Kim is getting married, and I need to be there for her, all smiles and support.

Once I grind some beans, I make a pot of strong coffee and eat something. Flipping on the music, I let the upbeat country tunes chase away my depressing memories and dance around the room. Today isn't about my past and regrets; it's about new beginnings.

Glancing at my phone, I scroll through a few messages. I'm taking a few weeks off from managing my business in town. The summer round of tourists will be coming in, but my store manager, Maya, is capable, so I don't need to fret over what happens while I'm away.

Peeking out the window, I can see it's a nice day. I dress in my leggings and sports bra, lace up my running shoes, and then step outside, eager for the familiar comfort of the trail.

As I jog, I catch glimpses of the river and the majestic mountains surrounding the area. I enjoy my business in town, but outside is where I find peace and can untangle my thoughts and soothe my restless soul. After tending to everyone else's needs, I'm looking forward to spending time hiking and camping alone.

After a hot shower, I take my time styling my hair into an updo, pinning the little flower rhinestones to the French twist in the back of my head. Then, I apply makeup, which is something I rarely wear.

One last look in the mirror to make sure everything is as it should be, and I'm ready to face the day. I grab my purse and garment bag and rush to my car. I'm running late, and there's still so much to do before the wedding.

* * *

God, I hope I can get through today without falling apart. I rush to the front door of my mother's B&B, hoping everything is perfect for Kim's big day. I dash into the house and run upstairs to the bedroom designated for bridesmaids. Treasa and Connie are already dressed and heading out the door when I walk in. They giggle, flowing past me.

Slipping into my Maid of Honor dress, I glance in the

mirror, taking a moment to appreciate the way the pale blue dress complements my body. At least my sister had the sense to not choose something God-awful for me to wear. I grin at the 'Smokey the Bear' tattoo on my arm. I know it will look silly in wedding photos, but I'm sure Kim won't mind.

Dashing around the backyard where all the wedding chaos is, I'm so wrapped up in my thoughts that I don't see him—until it's too late.

We collide, and I stumble backward. Before I can hit the ground, his hands catch me. Dazed, I look up into hazel eyes framed by the dark hair of a man dressed in a tailored suit. I suck in a breath. His handsome and unfamiliar face flickers with amusement.

"Oh, I'm so sorry!" My words tumble out in a quick apology. I turn to check the back of my dress to make sure I didn't get any dirt on it. Then I look up.

"No problem at all," he replies, flashing a smile. "I wasn't watching where I was going, either. I'm Mark, Mark Harrison."

Mustering a smile, I extend my hand out of courtesy. "Hi, I'm Amber Holloway, the bride's sister and Maid of Honor."

His handshake's warm, and I feel a strange connection. "I'm the Best Man. Nice to meet you, Amber." He doesn't let go, so I withdraw my hand.

"You must be Ethan's longtime friend. He mentioned you'd be flying in."

A smile widens on his face. One of his eyebrows arches slightly. "Ethan mentioned you, too."

"He did, did he?" I hope Ethan wasn't planning on setting us up. Though this guy's good-looking, and normally, I might enjoy getting to know him, I'm in no mood to deal with a man right now.

He chuckles, "It was all good."

"Well, I need to go. Nice meeting you." Glancing around, I search for an escape route, then spot Mom and head off in her direction.

When I get closer, I can't help but notice how her eyes are sparkling with joy. "Hi, Mom." I lean in and kiss her on the cheek.

"Does everything look okay?" she asks, scanning the area with a critical eye.

"Mom, your dress is perfect. And the arrangements, they're just flawless. You and Jess have outdone yourselves."

She lets out a soft sigh. "Kim wanted it to be casual, just family and close friends."

I touch her arm, imagining the guest list dilemma. "I bet you had a hard time figuring out who *not* to invite."

She nods. "Well, yes. I didn't want to snub anyone. But Ethan, bless his heart, only invited his friend Mark. I guess he's serious about starting a new life here with your sister. He is such a sweet man. I'm so glad everything worked out for them."

"Me too."

"How are you doing?" Her eyes search my face.

I muster a smile. "Okay," I reply, but inside I'm a wreck. "I want to go see Kim before the ceremony begins." I wave and slip away, looking for my sister.

As I navigate the area, my mind is a whirlwind of emotions. I take a deep breath and plaster on a smile just as Kim appears on the back porch. She's radiant, a vision of happiness.

I rush over. "Oh Amber, can you believe this is really happening?" Kim's voice is brimming with excitement, and her face is glowing. "I'm so glad you'll be by my side as my Maid of Honor. I know how hard this must be for you."

There is a pang in my heart, but I push it aside. "I wouldn't miss it for the world," I say, pulling her into a warm hug. "You deserve every bit of happiness after what you've been through."

"Bobby's thrilled he finally has a dad."

"I bet."

Stepping back, I allow myself to really look at her. The way the light plays off her hair, the sparkle in her eyes, the sheer happiness she radiates—it's almost too much. Envy flickers in me, but my overwhelming love and happiness for her overshadows it.

I glance around, taking in the simple yet beautiful decorations adorning the trees and chairs. White lights twist around the trunks of maple trees while mason jars filled with wildflowers hang from branches. More wildflowers decorate the end of each row of chairs. It looks like a scene right out of a Disney movie, and I can't help but feel bittersweet. I'm overjoyed for my sister, yet standing here surrounded by the picture-perfect yard, I can't ignore the one person missing today. It should've been our father walking Kim down the aisle on her wedding day. I imagine his face—crinkled with smile lines, blinking back proud tears. I don't know if we'll ever get over his loss. He was the pillar of our family. My older brother, Grady, has been trying to fill his shoes, but no one will ever live up to our dad's reputation.

My nephew, Bobby, comes strolling across the lawn, nearly knocking over a chair. He looks gangly and awkward in his suit, but his eyes shine with excitement. Kim's face lights up when she sees her son. She waves, and he comes over to join us.

"Oh, look at you! So handsome!" She pulls him in for a tight hug, which he accepts with a roll of his eyes. He has her soon-to-be husband's thick blond hair and smile.

The music changes then, signaling the start of the ceremony. Guests hurry to take their seats. "I guess we better go." I give Kim's arm a supportive squeeze before going down the stairs, dabbing at my eyes.

We take our positions, and I adjust the skirt of my dress again, trying to distract myself from the emotions welling inside me. Music is playing in the background.

As Ethan takes his place under the flowered arch, I watch him. His eyes are on Kim, swimming with warmth and tenderness. He looks at her like she hung the stars in the sky just for him. At this moment, I know my sister has found her soulmate.

The ceremony begins, and I walk down the aisle, keeping my emotions in check. After Grady hands over Kim to her groom, I take my place opposite Mark. He shoots me a flashy grin and winks. I give him a polite nod in return.

As they say their vows, I barely hear their words, lost in my own thoughts. Suddenly, everyone erupts with joy as Ethan kisses his new bride.

Then the toasts begin as family and friends pay tribute to my sister and praise Ethan for his desire to be part of the Leavenworth community. After my small speech of support and love, I'm vaguely present, just waiting for the speeches to end. And when they do, I make a beeline for the open bar at the reception.

Mark is at the bar, sipping his drink. He lights up when I join him. I grab a glass of champagne, while others head for the dance floor around me. I'm not sure if I should get drunk and make a fool of myself or discreetly leave. I give myself one hour to decide.

"So, quite a wedding, huh? The bride looks beautiful," Mark remarks, his gaze flicking toward Kim, who's getting hugs from our friends. I nod, feeling the corners of my mouth lift as

I watch my sister's joy radiating from her. "She does. She's truly happy now."

Mark edges closer. "And what about you? Any man you're dreaming of tying the knot with?"

My head shakes before I can even consider the question. I want to leave it at that. Let the subject drop before it digs too deep.

He leans back, assuming a casual air against the bar, that signature grin not budging an inch. "Marriage isn't for everyone you know—" His words trail off, and there's a pause, an assumption hanging between us. He chuckles then, breaking the brief silence. "Who would've thought those two would end up together, huh?"

"It seems it was destined to happen," I reply.

"For them, maybe. But why should the rest of us get tangled up in someone else's expectations?" He tosses back his drink.

"Is that how you view commitment?" I raise the glass to my mouth to hide my annoyance.

"He gave up his career for Kim, didn't he? I'd say that was quite a sacrifice."

I can't help but defend the truth I know. "From what I've heard, he wasn't happy with his success, and even less so without Kim."

Mark concedes with a nod. "You've got a point. I watched the toll it took on him. He suffered a lot. I just hope it was worth it."

I finish my glass of champagne. It's doing little to quell my feelings. "I was about to get married once," I say, the words suddenly spilling out, revealing my sadness. "He died before we had the chance. Since then, weddings ... are difficult for me."

I watch his expression change into genuine concern. "I'm sorry. That was thoughtless of me."

"It's fine," I say, eager to escape this conversation and the sympathy in his eyes.

But as I turn, he reaches out, touching my arm with a tenderness that halts me. "I really am sorry. I can be an idiot sometimes," he admits. "It sounds like you loved him deeply."

His sincerity catches me off-guard. "I did," I confess.

The air thickens with our shared silence, the weight of my past pressing down. It's Mark who breaks it. "I hate to see you looking so sad. How about one dance? No expectations, just a dance." He holds out his hand for me to take.

I hesitate, with a reluctant smile tugging at my lips. "Just one," I agree.

As the slow tune starts to play, he places one hand on my back and with the other holds my hand with unexpected gentleness, and I feel a flutter inside me. Our bodies move together with an ease that surprises me. I tell myself it's the rhythm of the dance that comforts me, not his arms. But as the music envelops us, for a fleeting moment, I let myself enjoy the warmth, the connection, the sense of being understood—even though I know I'll push it away as soon as the song ends.

"What do you do?" he asks. "For work, I mean."

"I own a boutique in town," I answer. "I sell clothes and gifts to tourists."

"Sounds quaint," he chuckles, and I can't help but bristle. I make darn good money from the people who come into my shop and buy stuff.

"And what about you?"

"I'm a real estate developer. I make deals and such. Don't worry, it's as boring as it sounds," he says with a smile.

"Are you so important that you'll be running off tomorrow to make a deal?"

He pulls me closer. "Hmm. I was actually thinking of sticking around a while after the wedding. Ethan mentioned there's a lot to see. Maybe you could show me some of the sights? We could go to dinner and get to know each other better."

The way he whispers this in my ear sends a clear message, one I'm not keen on entertaining. "I'm sure one of my brothers could play tour guide."

"I was hoping *you* would, actually."

"I have plans, sorry. Now, if you'll excuse me, I need to make the rounds."

As I slip away, I hear him murmur, "Independent ... I like that."

My brother Grady comes up behind me and gives me a hug. "How are you holding up?"

"I'm okay," I lie.

He smiles. "I guess I'll be next if I don't blow it."

"Yeah, if you don't blow it," I tease him.

"Have a little faith in me."

"I do." I kiss him on the cheek. "You and Jess make a great couple."

Just then, my other brother Matt shows up. "I'm glad this worked out for Kim. I still can't get over Ethan being the country music star Cody Williams and her keeping it a secret all these years."

"Yes." I swallow back my sadness. "They look happy."

Matt looks at me. "Are you okay, sis?"

I nod, but he wraps his arms around me and whispers, "You'll find another Prince Charming to live happily ever after with. I know it."

I let the tears fall, then sniff and wipe my face. "Thanks. I need another drink," I say, then walk away.

When Mark finds me later, he grabs my arm, and I turn and face him. "I owe you an apology. I got ahead of myself because, well, you're very attractive, and I got carried away."

Raising an eyebrow, I let him squirm. "Apology accepted."

He tries again, though. "Ethan suggested I take in the local sights. I heard you're the one to ask about outdoor adventures. Maybe you could show me the mountain trails?"

Before I can shut that down, Ethan appears, clapping a hand on Mark's shoulder. "Mark! So you've met my new sister-in-law."

"Yeah," Mark's smile is wide. "Amber just agreed to take me hiking."

I narrow my eyebrows and flash him a look. I didn't agree to drag him along on my hike. Alone time in the mountains is what I'm craving right now, not playing guide to a city slicker with a quick smile and too many lines.

Ethan's grin tells me he's unaware of the silent standoff, but I'm determined to set this straight. "I don't think Mark could keep up. Besides, I'm not just doing a day hike. I plan to be gone for several days. Maybe even a week if I feel like it."

Ethan laughs. "Give him a chance, Amber. He's my best friend. Can't you show Mark the views of the area while he's here? He'll only be in town for a little while."

"Okay," I mutter. "Consider it a wedding gift, then."

Chapter Two

Mark

I pull into the trailhead parking lot with the last of the supplies I snagged from the local outfitter in town. I kill the engine of my rental car and step out, the gravel crunching beneath my boots. It's a crisp morning and Amber's already geared up, leaning against her car like she's part of the scenery.

Going on this trip is a big deal for me. I've always been a loner, accustomed to relying on myself. Trusting strangers was never an option. Not when you learn early on that showing vulnerability can mean the difference between getting by and getting beaten down. But when my best friend Ethan asked me to be in his wedding, he also insisted I go for a hike with Amber, telling me I needed to experience a different side of life. One where I wasn't in control.

"Give me your phone," Amber says, with not a hint of greeting, just straight to the point.

I blink, surprised. "What?"

"I won't lead you into the mountains if you're going to be chained to that thing." She's serious, her hand outstretched, waiting.

"But what if something happens at the office and they need to reach me?" The words slip out before I can stop them, my mind racing with thoughts of missed emails and urgent calls.

"At the office?" She raises an eyebrow, a smirk dancing on her lips.

My cheeks burn with the realization that she's caught me. This is a vacation, I remind myself, a break from the relentless pace of the corporate world.

"No phone, no go." She's unwavering, hand still out.

Reluctantly, I dig into my vest pocket, feeling the smooth, familiar edges of the device that's become an extension of my hand. With a reluctant flick of my wrist, I hand it over. She takes it, holding it in her palm, almost ceremoniously, and locks it away in the back of her trunk, inside a metal box.

"You sure it's safe in there?" I can't help but ask, imagining my phone, my lifeline, locked away from the world.

"Safer than if I chuck it off the mountain." Her eyes twinkle with mischief.

"You wouldn't?" I'm half-joking, half-terrified of the answer.

She gives me a look with a smirk. "You don't know me very well, Mr. Harrison. I don't hike with people on their phones all the time. This trip is about enjoying nature."

A part of me wonders what I've gotten myself into. I'm already regretting spending several days with this strange woman who's as unpredictable as the trail ahead. I force a smile, and she seems satisfied, nodding once.

I lift the pack onto my back, the weight a sudden,

grounding reminder of what's coming. It's heavy, filled with necessities and a few comforts I wasn't willing to leave behind.

Amber sets off on the path without another word, and I fall in behind her. The trail is quiet except for the rustle of leaves and the crunch of our boots. I'm unsure if I should break the silence, so I don't say anything. My mind drifts to my business. I've got a big project I'm bidding on that I'm looking forward to when I get back. I begin running the details through my mind.

Not paying attention to where my feet are, I snag the toe of my boot on a tree root and lunge forward but catch myself before I fall.

Amber looks back. "You okay?"

"Yes." I cuss under my breath. This is Ethan's idea. He told me I needed a break before I burned out and that the great outdoors would help me refocus. I hope he's right. I want to be in top shape when I return to the office. I shove thoughts of work aside for the moment, focusing instead on the sway of Amber's hips and the path before us.

As I match my steps with Amber's on the ascending trail, her ease with the terrain irritates me. She strides like a mountain goat, and I'm struggling to keep up, sweating through my T-shirt. My breath's coming in heavy bursts. But Amber? She breathes like it's no big deal.

The view from up here is insane—the scenery that makes you forget the burn in your lungs, like some adventure movie set. I expect a bear to come charging out at any moment.

Amber stops. She turns to me, her face flushed with excitement. "Well, what do you think?"

Her joy is real, infectious even, and for a moment, I forget I'm about to pass out from the exertion.

Amber stretches her arms, and the sunlight catches her

silhouette against the backdrop of the mountains. Her hair dances in the breeze, illuminated by the golden rays, making it hard to focus on anything else. I tear my gaze away from her and turn my attention back to the view.

The mountains rise in layers of blue and green, their peaks disappearing into wisps of clouds. Below, Lake Wenatchee sparkles like a sapphire, its waters reflecting the sky above. I grin despite the burn in my legs and the ache in my lungs. "It's absolutely gorgeous," I reply, slightly breathless.

But despite the beauty surrounding us, it's Amber who captivates me. Her laughter echoes through the crisp air, blending with the rustle of leaves and the chirping of birds. At this moment, with her by my side, the world feels alive and vibrant in a way I've never experienced before.

Amber nods, and we take a moment to just stand there, basking in the dying light of the sun, painting the sky in shades of pink and purple.

"Just a bit farther," she says, and off she goes. I follow, wondering how much farther my legs can carry me.

Once we reach our campsite, and I collapse onto a log, my shirt sticks to me uncomfortably. Amber's got a sheen of sweat, but it looks sexy on her. The mountain air's cool, thin, and challenging to my lungs, which have grown too comfortable with indoor air and city smog. I watch as she slips off her pack with the ease of someone who's done this a thousand times.

She points to a spot nearby, and I nod. "Thanks," I grunt, already mapping out my plan of attack. The last time I set up a tent, I was at a camp for wayward boys.

Amber is in her element, tent pieces flying together like they're magnetized. I watch for a moment. My tent's in a neat, foreign pile on the ground.

Amber's gaze is on me as I lay out the pieces. The instructions are a crutch I toss aside—I won't need them. I can figure this out. With a sharp snap, I extend the first pole.

Amber raises an eyebrow.

"I'm fine," I say, more to myself than to her. A smirk curls the edge of her lips, and she steps back, giving me space to prove it.

I take the challenge head-on, piecing together the skeleton of my temporary home. It's not a textbook setup; there's more force than finesse, but the frame stands solid against the light breeze. After a stubborn struggle, the rain fly fabric's draped over now, too. It's not as neat as Amber's, but it's functional. "It'll hold," I say, placing my hands on my hips while admiring my accomplishment.

I catch her rolling her eyes. "Alright, hotshot. Firewood," she challenges, and I'm off, gathering what I need.

The wood catches quickly after I flick my lighter. "Natural talent," I say through the tears from the smoke, a cocky grin spreading on my face as I watch the flames dance.

"What did you bring to eat?" Amber asks. "You did remember to pack food, didn't you?"

"Of course." I show her what I brought—a bottle of wine, brie, caviar, a sleeve of artisan crackers, a jar of olives, some smoked salmon, antipasto, a loaf of French bread, some salami, and chocolate.

Amber's eyebrow arches at my display of provisions. "Well, I hope that provides you with enough energy out here."

"Hey, I didn't want to eat any freeze-dried junk."

Her smirk tells me she's not impressed.

As we settle in, I battle with the foldable chair I brought, which seems to have a personal vendetta against me.

Her amusement is clear as day, even as she tries to hide it.

"The man is useless," she mutters, but there's a teasing in her voice.

"I've got other skills," I reply. "They just don't involve tramping around in the woods."

"I'm sure you do." She laughs.

"Well, Amber," I say, a sly smile spreading across my face. "If you knew me better, you'd be impressed by what I can do."

She bursts out laughing.

"I may not know much about camping, but I do know a thing or two about surviving in the cutthroat business world."

"Oh, really?" There's a hint of challenge in her voice. "I didn't realize that sitting in a cushy office all day was equivalent to surviving in the wilderness."

Sitting in the office all day? Sitting in an airplane is more like it. I don't back down. "Hey, it's not easy out there in the business world," I say, my voice rising. "You have to be tough, resilient, and adaptable to make it."

"Hah! In case you forgot, I have a business too."

"Oh? That little gift shop in town?" I regret my tone as soon as I say that.

Amber glares at me, her eyes narrowing. "It's a small business that I've worked hard to build and maintain. Just because it's not some big corporate enterprise doesn't mean it's not important."

"Hey, I'm not saying your business isn't important," I tell her, trying to backpedal. "I'm just saying that it's not exactly the same as running a large company."

"You know, Mark, not everyone measures success by the size of their ... bank account," she says. "Some of us value community, creativity, and making a difference in the world."

I can't help but roll my eyes at her idealistic tone. "Yeah, yeah, save the world and all that." My voice is dripping with sarcasm. "But at the end of the day, you still have to pay the bills." It's a good thing she has no idea how rich I am. She'd have a hell of a lot more respect if she knew how hard I worked to get there. But I'm not going to bring it up. She wouldn't understand. She's a tree hugger, after all.

"Survival here depends on being prepared to deal with the unexpected. Weather, change in terrain, physical endurance, and dealing with wildlife. Doesn't matter how wealthy you are; people disappear all the time up here in the mountains. If you were out here alone, do you have anyone at home who would be crying if you didn't come back?"

That stung. She has a point. I have one person who I could call a true friend, and he just married Amber's sister.

"I'm not an idiot. I could figure it out."

"Oh?" She smirks.

We sit in silence. Thoughts whirl around my head. Amber doesn't know the half of it. Growing up poor in Chicago, I learned early on that you must be tough to survive. With a single mom struggling to make ends meet on welfare, I spent more time on the streets than at home. She worked odd jobs under the table to bring in extra cash, doing whatever it took to keep the lights on. But it was never enough.

I wore hand-me-down clothes that didn't fit right and often went to bed hungry. The hunger was the worst part. That empty, gnawing feeling in my gut made it hard to focus in school. Not that school mattered much, anyway. The teachers had all but given up on kids like me. What future could a poor kid from my part of town really have?

So, I made my own future. I studied books about business at the library. I started selling anything I could get my hands on —candy, shoes, small electronics, whatever would turn a profit. I quickly learned that on the streets, money equals power and respect. So, I hustled day and night, determined to make something of myself. By fifteen, I had a network of suppliers and customers across three neighborhoods. I even took the bus downtown some days to try my luck in richer territory.

Sure, I got roughed up by local gang members now and then. But I was fast on my feet and even faster with my mouth. I could talk my way out of almost anything. And the money I was making, the power I held in my community, offered its own kind of protection that no one could take from me.

My street smarts and business savvy were the tickets out of that life. The day I graduated high school, I drove off in a second-hand luxury car I fixed up. A few days later, I drove it straight to the real estate office I had scouted downtown and demanded an internship. They saw the hunger in my eyes and decided to take a chance.

The rest is history, as they say. I out-hustled those real estate vets right from the start. Before long, I was running my own small firm, then a bigger one. Now, I'm one of the biggest developers in the country. Everything I have, I earned with grit, brains, and determination.

So, if Amber thinks I couldn't make it a week in her precious mountains, she's got another think coming. I've survived worse and fought harder battles than this terrain could ever throw at me. Her world may be miles apart from the streets I come from. But if she thinks I couldn't handle myself out here alone, she just revealed her own ignorance. My past has given me strength and resilience that her small-town privileged self could never understand.

I finish off my smoked salmon and crackers. The sky is dark with clouds, and I hear a rumbling in the background, and I'm beat.

"Well, I'm going to lay out my sleeping bag." I go to my

tent. Inside, I look around. *It's the size of a damn doghouse.* I roll out the thing and plop down. It's hard as a rock, but at the moment, I don't care. As soon as I close my eyes, I'm out.

I wake to drips hitting me in the face. *Crap.* I squint as the next drip lands on my forehead. My tent is leaking.

The rain is coming down hard as I stand shivering outside Amber's tent. My sleeping bag is wrapped around me like a cocoon, but it does little to stop the cold from seeping into my bones.

"Amber," I call out, my teeth chattering. "I've got a problem."

"Fix it yourself," comes her muffled reply.

"It's raining, and my damn tent is leaking," I say. "I'm soaked."

I hear her let out an exaggerated sigh before she unzips her tent flap and peers out at me. I must look pathetic, standing dripping wet and shivering uncontrollably.

"Get in," she says, sounding annoyed.

"Thanks." I scramble into the warm, dry sanctuary of her tent. "Got a heater in here?" I joke lamely, trying to lighten the mood.

She just glares at me.

"Put your sleeping bag down in the corner. I don't want you getting the inside of my tent all wet."

Amber starts to unzip her sleeping bag and pats its empty half. "Come on, get in here. It's warmer if we share."

I smile at the invite. When I drop my sleeping bag, she can see I'm just wearing tight boxer briefs.

She shoots me an annoyed look. "If you had brought some thermal underwear, they could have kept you warmer."

"Hey, it's my first time." I grin, rubbing my hands together, hoping to spark her interest. "I know just the thing to warm me up."

She shakes her head and mutters, "Don't even try or you'll be sleeping in the rain."

I slide into her sleeping bag beside her, acutely aware of how close we are. I can feel the heat from her body radiating into mine, like a warm blanket encircling us both, and I quit shivering. She's tucked some kind of makeshift barrier between us, but it's so thin that we might as well be pressed against each other.

I lay there, just listening to the rain drumming against her tent. But the sound of her breathing starts to change, and I realize she's asleep.

I turn to face her and notice how beautiful Amber looks, even in the dim light of the tent. She has nice features—a turned-up nose, high cheekbones, and her full lips are slightly parted as she breathes. Oh, to kiss those lips. To make love to her gorgeous body. *Damn.* I better not think about that right now, or I'll get myself into trouble.

I daydream, wondering what it would be like to take her away from here. To fly her across the ocean and show her the view from the Eiffel Tower or hills above the vineyards of Tuscany or the mountains in Switzerland. *Who am I kidding?* She has no interest in a guy like me or my lifestyle. I roll over, trying to ignore that she's so close, yet so far away.

I wake to Amber gently shaking my shoulder. "Rise and shine, city boy," she says in a chipper voice. "Time to break camp."

I groan and rub my eyes. My body aches from yesterday's hike and the night cramped in Amber's sleeping bag. I crawl out of the tent, immediately missing its warmth. The morning air is frigid and damp. Amber is already dressed. I scramble to my tent and get dressed, thankful that my clothes are dry.

I pull out some French bread and tear off a bite with my teeth. When she looks at me, I make a face and growl, "Grrr."

She rolls her eyes. "You'll need more than that." She hands me a bowl of oatmeal and I choke it down, followed by instant coffee.

"Let's get moving. I want to cover some ground before the rain starts up again." She's packing up her gear with practiced efficiency.

I fumble around, trying to roll up my soggy sleeping bag. Amber watches me struggle for a minute before stepping in.

"Here, you have to squeeze the air and water out as you roll," she demonstrates. In seconds, she has my sleeping bag packed up neatly.

I feel useless watching her nimble hands work. She runs circles around me when it comes to this outdoor stuff. I don't like relying on anyone, especially a woman.

Then we hit the trail again. The exertion helps warm my stiff muscles. Amber sets a brisk pace. But after yesterday, I'm determined to keep up. I try to appreciate the natural splendor surrounding us. Still, my mind keeps drifting back to my over-flowing inbox and looming deadlines. Business is my life, not gallivanting in the woods.

Yet, seeing Amber so at peace in this environment makes me envy her appreciation for life's little pleasures. Finally, I ask, "So, what do you do besides hike in your spare time?"

Amber glances back with a smile. "A lot of things. I go to musical productions and plays."

I raise my eyebrows. "There are cultural activities in Leavenworth?"

"We aren't as backward as you might think," she chuckles. "There are several great restaurants around, like the Wildflour."

"The Wildflour? Sounds like a place that serves salads with names I can't pronounce," I joke.

She laughs. "No, they make their own pasta and have excellent food."

"I love authentic Italian pasta."

"Their pasta is a bit more creative than marinara sauce on noodles.

"What do you expect from me? I'm Italian. I'm set in my ways on some things."

"Really?" Amber looks genuinely surprised. "Ever tried anything different?"

I chuckle. "Does hiking in the woods count?"

She laughs. "Maybe you need an outdoor hobby to get you out of your sedentary life. Ever thought about whitewater rafting or rock climbing?"

"Rock climbing?" I picture myself dangling from a cliff. "I take other types of risks." Then I think about piloting my plane and how much I enjoy soaring above the clouds.

She grins. "You could take up bird watching."

"Bird watching?" I pretend to be interested. "I'm a pro at that. I can tell a pigeon from a crow."

Amber's laughter rings through the trees, and for a moment, I forget about the stiffness in my muscles and the trail under my feet. We continue our hike, the conversation flowing more easily now as if the wilderness is slowly chipping away at the walls I've built around myself.

We continue upward and the thin air starts to burn my lungs. I'm drenched in sweat but bursting with accomplishment when we finally reach the summit. At a clearing, we stop to take in the view. Lush green valleys and snow-capped peaks sprawl out before us. Amber closes her eyes and takes a deep breath. "Moments like this are why I come here."

"That's an amazing view," I say between gulps of water.

"You made it!"

We high-five to celebrate the moment.

As we begin our descent, dark clouds roll in. Amber's pace quickens. "We need to find shelter before this storm hits," she says.

The first raindrops start pelting us as we half-jog down the rocky path. Thunder rumbles overhead. Amber leads us off the trail toward a small cave carved into the mountainside.

We duck inside just as the downpour begins. It's a tight squeeze, and I'm hyper-aware of Amber's body pressed against mine. My heart hammers in my chest, and all I can think about is how much I want to wrap my arms around her.

"Cozy, huh?" she jokes.

I let out a nervous laugh. "Yeah, real cozy."

We stand in awkward silence, listening to the storm raging outside. I sneak glances at Amber, thinking how, under different circumstances, I'd be turning on the charm, hoping to convince her I could give her a night to remember.

After what feels like an eternity, the rain lets up. We head back to the trail, the tension between us dissipating along with the clouds.

By the time we set up camp, I'm spent. My feet throb as I kick off my boots. Amber gets a fire going and heats up some stew, which she offers me. We eat in tired silence.

As the last of the daylight fades, we crawl into our tents. I'm out as soon as my head hits the pillow.

* * *

I wake before sunrise to Amber calling my name. "Time to head out."

I groan, but her enthusiasm convinces me to haul myself out of my sleeping bag.

As I emerge from the tent, the first hints of dawn light filter through the tall pines surrounding our camp. The air is crisp and cool, scented with pine and soil. It's so quiet this early. The only sound is the soft rustling of squirrels scampering up nearby trunks. One pauses on a branch, eyeing me with its beady gaze, then continues on its way.

I stretch, my joints cracking. Sleeping in a sleeping bag on the hard ground isn't my thing. But as the sky glows pink on the horizon, I experience a rare sense of peace. I've always been an early riser, though usually to the sound of the radio blasting rather than songbirds.

As sunlight fills our camp, other forest sounds emerge. I hear the buzz of flying insects dancing over the stream beside our tents and chipmunks skittering through the underbrush. Then, an occasional far-off call of a hawk. Strangely, the internal soundtrack constantly filling my mind has gone quiet this morning. For once, I feel fully present. I glance around. Dew glitters like diamonds on the ferns and mosses covering the forest floor. A light breeze brings the sweet scent of wild-flowers down from the meadows above. I breathe deeply, filling my lungs with crisp, pine-scented air. No car exhaust or garbage smells, just earthy purity.

Realizing Amber has already started making breakfast, I walk over to help. Once I've finished my scrambled eggs and coffee, I rinse the dishes. After that, I shoulder my heavy pack, ready to embrace the challenge of another day in Amber's domain.

Chapter Three

Amber

Mark's a piece of work. He must be so rich he has someone wipe his butt for him. I don't know why I agreed to take him on this trip. Then I smile, feeling grateful for the chance to share this experience with him, even if he is a bit of a camping disaster. It must be a humbling experience for someone like him. He obviously isn't used to feeling so out of control. I get there's a first time for everything.

Today, Mark's got two left feet. I worry he'll stumble on the trail and go sliding down the mountainside. I don't want to deal with trying to rescue him if he does.

We stop several times for water and a bite of a granola bar.

"I don't know why people eat these things," Mark complains. "They taste awful."

"Well, Mark, maybe if you weren't used to eating caviar and

champagne every day, your taste buds wouldn't be so spoiled," I tease.

Mark lets out a chuckle, "Touché, Amber."

"These bars give you the energy you need to make it up this mountain."

Mark scowls and mutters something under his breath as he takes another bite of the bar.

You'd think I asked him to eat a piece of wood by his expression. "You know, if you want to quit, go ahead. There are restaurants in town. I'm sure you'll have no trouble finding your way out of here," I joke.

Mark shoots me a look of annoyance. "Ha, Ha, very funny."

"Mark, I'm sorry. It's just that I'm used to doing this kind of thing."

Mark nods. "Yeah, I know. Sorry for sounding like a jerk. Believe it or not, being out here is starting to grow on me."

I smile, feeling relieved that he isn't completely hating the trip.

"I never thought I'd be doing something like this. Camping, I mean," he tells me. "I'm glad I came."

* * *

After another less strenuous hike, I pick a place for us to camp. I try to hide my smile as I watch Mark fumble with the tent poles again. Something is endearing about seeing him so focused on figuring it out. He's trying. I have to give him that.

The exertion brought a sheen of sweat to Mark's brow. "I think I'll go clean up before dinner."

I nod, watching him pull off his shirt and head toward the creek. Alone now, I start gathering kindling and logs for the fire. The familiar tasks soothe me, allowing my mind to wander.

By the time Mark returns, I have a respectable blaze going. I'm suddenly very aware of his physical presence. He looks refreshed, his hair damp from the creek. I swear he wants me to notice him as he pulls on a sweatshirt over his broad chest. I shake my head. Yeah, I have to admit, he's one hot looking guy.

I cook a simple meal over the fire for us as the darkness grows.

"So, Amber, why did you choose Leavenworth of all places to open a shop?"

I look up at Mark, trying to gauge his interest. "I grew up here," I reply. "So, it just made sense to open a shop in my hometown. Leavenworth is a popular tourist destination. It's the perfect place for a gift shop."

Mark nods, but I can tell he still doesn't quite understand. "I like it here. It's a beautiful place to live, and it's nice knowing I have family and friends nearby."

Mark twists a pine branch in his hand. "Ethan mentioned that your family's pretty close. I guess your sister really impressed him."

"Yeah, I suppose she did." I push off from the tree, taking a step closer. "You've been friends with Ethan for a while, I take it."

Mark nods, a distant look in his eyes as if he's sifting through his memories. "Yeah, we've had each other's back for a long time. I was there when he was playing gigs anywhere they'd let him set up a mic. We met not long after he and Kim ... you know, after they broke up. I watch him rise and crash and then get up again. I pressured him to go into rehab and do what he needed to do to get his life back on track." There's a note of pride in his voice. "But through it all, he never really got over your sister. It was a curse, I suppose."

"What?" My eyebrows shoot up.

"Loving someone that much."

The campfire crackles, its glow painting shadows on his face as he feeds another log to the flames. I'm curious about why he would think love is a curse. "What about you, Mark? Have you ever been in love?"

He pauses, a flicker of something unreadable crossing his face. "Me?" he replies, sounding on edge. "I'm not the relationship type."

I study him, the way he avoids my gaze. "Why? Did someone break your heart?"

He chuckles. "You'd be surprised to know I was married once."

I lean forward, intrigued. "Oh? What happened?"

He tosses another stick into the fire, watching it catch. "It was a disaster. We fought all the time." He lets out a heavy sigh. "Turns out she was more interested in my bank account that me."

"Did you love her?"

He shrugs, a half-smile playing on his lips. "Love?" Then he laughs. "Certainly not the kind Ethan and Kim have. Veronica was fun for a while, but ... there was never that deep connection people talk about. She was very competitive, and we were always at odds. After a while, I grew tired of her game, so I ended it. She was bitter about the divorce and took a chunk of my earnings when she left."

I nod. "I'm sorry, but I guess that's bound to happen in your world."

He looks up with a hard expression. "What do you mean?"

I hesitate, then decide to be honest. "You live in a world

where everyone is jockeying for power and pretends to be something else. They never get close to anyone because they're scared to show who they really are."

He snorts, tossing a pinecone into the flames. "You don't know what you're talking about. No one is honest. They're all out for themselves."

"Pity," I murmur, feeling a sudden sadness for him. "It must be pretty lonely believing that."

He stares at me with an intense gaze. "If you believe in honesty, tell me something you've never told anyone before."

I look away. The surrounding forest is quiet. "Sometimes I get scared when I'm fighting fires," I tell him.

He does a double take. "Fighting fires? I thought you ran a gift shop."

"I do," I admit, meeting his gaze again. "But I volunteer during the summer season if a wildfire breaks out and they need help. It's important to me."

He nods, visibly impressed. "Never met a woman fire-fighter before."

I smile, warmed by his approval. "Your turn. Tell me something personal that people don't know about you."

He clears his throat, looking uncomfortable. "I grew up poor. My mom worked when I was young. But gave up when juggling different jobs became too hard on her and went on welfare."

I can't hide my surprise. "I would've never guessed."

"Yeah," he says, his voice sounding bitter. "After that, she never missed an opportunity to take advantage—of the system or the generosity of others."

I sense a deep pain in him. "Do you still talk to her?"

He looks into the fire, his face unreadable. "She passed away years ago from an opioid overdose."

I want to reach out to offer some kind of comfort, but I hold back. "Siblings?" I ask softly.

The cloud in his eyes darkens. "You don't have to tell me," I add quickly, not wanting to push him.

He smiles, but it's hollow. "It's fine." He flits his eyes over to me. "You're not going to sell this to the tabloids, are you?"

I shake my head. "No, of course not."

He sighs, the sound mingling with the crackling of the fire. "I was born Mario Vitale. I changed my name when I turned eighteen. Wanted to start fresh. To never look back. My brother's in jail for murder."

I swallow hard. The night's suddenly colder than a moment ago. "I'm sorry."

"Don't be. He deserved what he got. He was robbing a store. The guy didn't need to die over a damn TV."

We sit in silence for a moment, letting everything he just told me sink in. I'd misjudged him, assuming he came from a life of sophistication, wealth, and privilege.

When I shiver, he moves closer, draping his jacket over my shoulders. His hand brushes my neck, and I suppress a sigh.

"The stars are incredible out here," he murmurs, glancing up at the velvety sky dotted with a million pricks of light.

"No light pollution," I reply softly. We sit in contented silence for a while. The only sound is the crackling of the fire.

I know I should turn in, but I'm reluctant to get up. Mark's arm encircles me, his body radiating warmth in the cooling night air. Being this close to him awakens my senses and makes me hyperaware of each subtle movement.

The light dances across Mark's features. I can see the Italian in him—dark hair, olive skin, chiseled jaw—unmistakably handsome. Several times, I notice his gaze lingering on me. The energy between us is electric and primal.

"It feels strange out here," he says.

"What do you mean?" I turn and find myself looking deep into his eyes.

"I don't know. Special. Like we are the only two people on this mountain." His eyes drop as his mouth hovers near mine, and I swallow hard.

I stir, sliding out from under his jacket. "We should get some rest," I say, breaking the spell. "We've got an early start tomorrow."

He nods, his eyes focused on my face. "Good night, Amber."

In my tent, I replay those moments by the fire, my skin still tingling from his touch. As I drift off, I see his face behind my eyelids. It's the last image before sleep claims me.

Chapter Four

Mark

I can't take my eyes off Amber as we hike along the ridge. She's a far cry from the glossy, high-maintenance women I'm used to. Amber's beauty is different; it's dynamic and real. No fillers or enhancements. She's the total package of natural beauty, strength, and persistence all rolled into one.

But it's not just her body that draws me to her. It's who she is on the inside. I smile as she hums to herself when she's walking, and I look when she points out the footprints of the different wildlife, explaining to me what animal made them.

"Don't you get bored in your shop doing the same thing all the time?" I ask.

She pauses and turns to me. "Why would you think that? I get to meet so many interesting people. Sure, sometimes we get the typical tourist crowd, but there are also a lot of backpackers and outdoor enthusiasts who wander into my store.

"One time, I met a German couple planning to hike the entire Pacific Crest. We ended up chatting for over an hour! They promised to send me a postcard from Canada when they finished the trail. Moments like those make the chaos of owning a small business totally worth it."

I watch a nostalgic smile creep across her face as she shares more stories.

"I've had tourists from Europe, Asia, Australia—you name it. They all want a little piece of Leavenworth to bring home."

"Why Leavenworth?"

She pauses and turns to me, her blue eyes dancing. "You wouldn't believe Leavenworth in the winter and holiday season. People flock from all over to see our little Bavarian village all lit up. There are carolers singing in the gazebo, and musicians playing around town. Everyone is dressed in colorful hats and scarfs. Kids are having fun sledding in the park. We even have a store dedicated to Christmas ornaments and another with nutcrackers.

"My store is filled with shoppers from morning to night searching for the perfect gift while the snow falls outside. It's like being in another world."

I try to envision the quaint downtown covered in snow with twinkling lights hanging from the trees, along with garlands and wreaths adorning the buildings. "Is it chaotic with the crowds?" I ask.

She laughs. "Oh yes, completely crazy, but wonderful! I have extra staff to help manage all the customers. We wrap gifts, help people put together gift baskets, and make recommendations. Everyone is just so festive and happy. It's my absolute favorite time of year."

I love seeing her passion bubble up as she describes it.

"And what do you do for fun in the winter? To get away from the crowds, I mean."

"Lots of things. Once there's enough snowpack, I ski and snowshoe. I snowmobile a lot, too. Some years, my brother Matt and I go out into the backcountry. Other times, we stick closer to home. But it's our favorite thing—racing through fresh powder, seeing wildlife. It's magical."

I shake my head. She seems fearless in this environment.

Amber pauses, taking a long drink from her water bottle, and I glimpse her profile against the vanilla clouds. Her skin glows, and her dark hair wisps lightly in the mountain breeze.

I'm captivated by her in a way I've never experienced before. My interactions with women have always been superficial, but with Amber, things feel different. I find myself longing to make her smile, hear her laughter, and be the reason her eyes light up. For the first time, I want to truly know someone. Something is going on inside me I don't quite understand. I'm hoping it isn't just being here in the mountains that makes me feel this way.

As we continue our hike, the view opens to a burst of colors in a meadow. I glance over at Amber, her hair catching the sunlight. "What's your favorite flower?" I ask, nodding toward the wildflowers dancing in the gentle breeze.

She looks at the meadow, then back at me with a thoughtful expression. "I don't know."

I probe a little further, trying to get a clearer picture. "Red roses? Most women like red roses."

"No. Pink," she replies with a soft smile.

I decide to shift gears. "What's your favorite movie?"

"Lion King," she says without hesitation.

"Lion King?" That answer is a surprise.

"Yeah. I like Disney movies." There's a hint of defensiveness in her voice.

"Why Disney movies?" I ask, genuinely interested.

"Because they're fun and they have happy endings. What about you?"

I think for a moment. "I'm more of an action movie guy. Matrix, Bond movies, Tom Cruise movies."

"Just like my brothers—super macho men movies." She grins. "I bet you've never watched a Disney movie."

"You're right. I don't have any kids, so there's no reason to."

"Would you like to have kids someday?"

I stop and look at her, and I don't know what to say. My dad abandoned our family when I was young, and I sure as hell wouldn't want to put the responsibility of raising my kid alone on any woman. I respond, "I think that would require me being in a committed relationship, and I'm not sure what kind of father I would be if I had a kid."

"Well, I come from a big family, and when I finally settle down, I want a bunch of kids."

The thought of having a family scares the heck out of me.

As we walk, the conversation flows to music.

"Who are your favorite singers?" she asks.

"Cody Williams is up there at the top," I answer.

"That's Ethan," she points out, a playful glint in her eyes.

"Yeah, I know," I reply, chuckling. "I was one of the few people who knew Cody Williams was Ethan's stage name. What about you?"

"I like Adele and Taylor Swift, and my sister Kim, of course." Her voice is full of pride when she mentions her sister.

I nod, thinking about her choices. "Color?" I ask, looking for another piece of her puzzle.

"Green. Because it is the color of life," she says, scanning the trees around us.

"Hmm. Mine is blue. Like the color of your eyes." The words slip out before I can stop them.

She laughs. "Chocolate?"

"Yes. Dark," I answer.

"I like chocolate caramels," she says, and I can almost taste the sweetness on her lips.

"Cookies?"

"Mom makes the best chocolate chip ones. Never found any I like better."

I can't help but imagine a cozy kitchen filled with the smell of baking and the warmth of family like I've seen in the movies. There is a pang of something akin to envy mixed with a deepening curiosity about this woman who loves Disney movies, green for its representation of life, and her mother's chocolate chip cookies.

"Nightgown or nude?" I grin.

"Wouldn't you like to know," she replies.

I laugh.

"I hope you aren't going to digress into asking me about my sex life next. Because that's personal."

"Okay. I'll stop now."

After a while, the terrain levels out, and Amber gestures for us to set up camp. I smile to myself as I put together my tent. I wonder if I can carry this feeling back down the mountain and into my everyday life.

Tonight, after we finish dinner, I pull out the bottle of wine I brought along with me. We'll be heading back tomorrow. Amber looks at me skeptically as I pour each of us a cup. "I just thought that it would be nice to have a little celebration," I say, offering her one.

I raise my cup. "To my camping experience and to my wonderful guide."

Amber "clinks" mine, takes a sip, then sets down her cup and stares at me.

"Mark, I didn't really want you to come hiking with me. I was depressed after Kim's wedding and was hoping this trip would help me get my life back on track. But I'm glad I brought you along."

"I'm sorry. I didn't realize that when I forced you to take me on this hike," I tell her.

Amber smiles. "It's okay. Your presence lifted my spirits. Not everyone is an outdoorsy type. But I'm glad you gave it a shot, and I hope you can take something positive away from the experience."

"Yes. It opened me up to something I never expected," I tell her.

As the evening continues, we drink more wine, and Amber loosens up. She laughs, and I become less guarded. We talk about the sights we've seen on this trip, and I feel sad it's coming to a close.

The fire crackles beside us. Her eyes hold a soft glow, reflecting the dancing flames. She tilts her head back, laughing at a clumsy joke I made about a squirrel we saw earlier. I can't help but smile, watching her.

I lean back and look up. The stars above are like a tapestry of light, so different from the city sky. "You know, I've never seen stars like these back home," I say, my voice softer than I intend. "I guess I never really took time to look at them before. In fact, I never really thought much about what it would be like hiking in the mountains before, either."

Our hands brush as we both reach for the wine, and something ignites inside of me.

The wood crumbles into the flames, a reminder that time is passing and that this moment is just that—a moment in my life that will soon end.

I reach out, gently tucking a strand of hair behind her ear. Her skin is soft, and she leans slightly into my touch. "You are really an amazing woman," I tell her.

She bites her lower lip and blushes. "You don't have to flatter me, Mark."

I shake my head. "I mean it. I'm glad you shared this time with me," I continue, feeling a sense of gratitude, and something deeper.

"Thanks."

The fire crackles between us. I take a deep breath, bolstered by the wine and the night's serenity. "I hope you don't find me so repulsive that you wouldn't consider seeing me again."

Her eyebrows rise, and there's an amused expression on her face. "Are you asking me out, Mark?"

Suddenly, I'm nervous and feel exposed—not like the confident man I project. "Yes, I am."

"I thought you were only here on vacation."

She's right. This trip was supposed to be a brief escape from my relentless routine, a temporary departure from my reality. But as I sit here, I realize that what I've found with Amber isn't something I want to leave behind. "Yes, but I can come back and visit," I say, surprising even myself with the earnestness in my voice.

"I don't know. I don't want to be just another conquest."

Her words hit me harder than I expect, and I wince. I should have never told her about my dating habits. "I understand," I admit, feeling a vulnerability I'm not accustomed to. "But getting to know you on this trip ... it's the closest I've ever felt to a woman. That should account for something, right?"

She takes a sip from her cup, her gaze lost in the flames. "I'll have to think about it," she finally says.

I dig through my pocket and pull out a crumbled business card. "If you change your mind, call me, okay? I'll make arrangements to fly out to visit you."

She takes the card and shoves it into her back pocket.

We finish our wine in comfortable silence, the night wrapping around us like something magical. Retreating to our separate tents, I lie awake, thoughts of Amber swirling in my mind —leaving her and this mountain without exploring what we've started is unbearable.

Determined, I quietly go out into the cool night air. My heart races as I gently unzip her tent flap and crawl inside. Amber's asleep, her face peaceful in the dim light of the moon filtering through the tent's fabric. My hands find a place on either side of her shoulders, anchoring me in this moment of uncertainty and longing. I lean in, close enough to watch her breath, the subtle rise and fall of her chest. Her features are relaxed, unguarded in sleep, and I'm struck by a deep, unspoken connection.

I lower my face toward hers, my pulse racing. My eyes trace the gentle curve of her lips and the soft flutter of her eyelids. I'm overwhelmed by the need to kiss her and close the space separating us.

As my lips touch hers, it's a soft, hesitant brush, a question waiting for an answer. She stirs beneath me, her eyes fluttering open. They meet mine, and in their depths, I see a mixture of surprise and something warmer, something inviting. Her eyes shine with unspoken emotions. We're both a little intoxicated, not just from the wine but from the spell of this night.

She smiles, and it's like a signal, a green light I've been waiting for.

My lips find hers again, this time with more urgency, more certainty. She responds, her arms winding around me, pulling me closer. Our kiss deepens, our tongues exploring each other with a hunger that seems to have been building since we first met. In this moment, nothing else matters—just Amber, the wilderness, and me.

I let my hand slip under her top, gasping at the warmth of her skin beneath my fingertips. Desire courses through me, a tidal wave of need and want. Her skin is so soft, so inviting, and I find myself lost in the sensation. I can feel the electricity between us, and I know that our time together is far from over.

I trail kisses along her neck. "Let's not think about tomorrow," I whisper, my heart in my throat. "Let's just be here, now, together." My voice is a mix of desire and hope, a plea for her to feel the same.

But then she pauses, her hand resting on mine, gently but firmly stopping my advance. "I'm sorry, Mark. I can't do this. You're leaving," she breathes out, her voice heavy with a mix of regret and resolve.

I lean down, trying to capture her lips again to sway her decision. "Please, I want us to remember this night for a long time," I murmur against her mouth.

But she's firm, pulling back slightly. "No, Mark. It's best if we don't take this any further."

Disappointment washes over me, a cold contrast to the heat of a moment ago. "Are you sure?" I ask, though I know the answer.

"Sorry," she whispers, and there's a finality in her voice that tells me she's made up her mind. "I need more than you can give me."

I drop my head. She's right. Amber's not looking for a one-night stand. Besides, she deserves someone who's going to stick around. Someone who will be there for her, not running off to meetings all the time. I take a deep breath, trying to calm the storm of emotions inside me. I lean in one last time, pressing a gentle kiss to her forehead before rolling off her.

I lay there for a moment, the weight of what could have been pressing down on me. With a heavy heart, I crawl out of her tent into the night, into a world that suddenly feels colder. *What the hell is happening to me out here? Why am I so taken by this woman?*

Chapter Five

Mark

Grabbing my clothes and towel, I head over to the stream. There, I splash cold water on my body and face. Swatting at a mosquito, I notice something feels different this morning. The usual chatter of birds is absent. In its place is an unsettling silence. I pause to take in my surroundings. The tall pines stand motionless, backlit by the rising sun. Their shadows stretch across the forest floor. In the distance, a light gray tendril is sliding low over the underbrush.

I breathe in the familiar earthy scents of moss and damp soil. Then I catch a whiff of something else—a sharp, acrid smell drifting through the forest. I know it isn't coming from our campsite. I scan the horizon, but there's no sign of where the odor's coming from. My senses are on high alert as I walk back to the campsite.

The smell is growing stronger, and now, a plume of smoke

is rising in the distance below us. My heart's racing, a mix of adrenaline and fear. "Amber," I call out, uncertain of what to do.

She's standing there, staring into the distance, her face pale and eyes wide. Something's not right. "Amber!" I repeat, more urgently.

She doesn't respond, just keeps staring, lost in some distant thought or memory. I step closer, waving my hand in front of her face. "Hey, are you okay?" I ask, my worry growing.

There's no reaction, just a vacant stare. I remember hearing about how people can freeze in emergencies, but I've never seen it firsthand. I need to snap her out of it, fast.

Gently, I grasp her shoulders. "Amber, talk to me. What should we do now?" I keep my voice calm but firm, trying to penetrate whatever fog she's lost in.

Slowly, her focus returns, her eyes meeting mine. There's a flicker of recognition, then alarm, as she takes in the situation. "Fire," she whispers in a shaky voice.

"Yeah. Fire," I reply, keeping my hold on her shoulders. "We need to move. Can you walk?"

She nods, steadying herself, and I can see her drawing on her inner strength. "Yes, I can walk."

"Good. Let's grab our stuff and get out of here." I keep one eye on her as we quickly pack our gear. As I strap on my backpack, a plume of smoke mushrooms upward in the sky.

The urgency of the situation is clear, but so is the need to keep Amber grounded. With shaking hands, Amber pulls out a phone I didn't know she had and calls for emergency help. She explains the situation to the operator and our location. After ending the call, she turns to me. "We have to get to the rescue site."

Amber thrusts a handkerchief at me. "Tie this around your mouth," she orders.

As we sprint down the mountain, my mind races. The forest now feels like a maze, with only one exit—through the fire below.

Amber's determination spurs me on. My feet stumble over rocks, but I push through, driven by the need to make sure Amber's safe and to get out of here.

As Amber and I hustle through the thickening smoke, I can't help but notice her determined strides, her resilience shining through despite the earlier moment of vulnerability. It's a stark reminder of why I admire her—she's strong, but even the strongest among us can have moments of weakness.

Up ahead, we encounter a group of hikers. I can tell they're lost, unsure of what to do next.

"Hey, everyone," I say, trying to sound confident. "We need to move quickly. The fire's spreading, and it's not safe here."

A young woman with blonde hair steps forward. "We don't know which way to go," she says, trembling. "We're all from out-of-town and ..."

I cut her off gently, "Don't worry, we'll figure this out together. The first thing is to stay calm." I look around, trying to get a sense of our surroundings through the smoke. "We need to head down the mountain."

A man with a long beard and a baseball cap nods in agreement. "He's right. We need to move now."

I turn to Amber. "Can you show us where to go? I'll bring up the rear, make sure no one falls behind."

She nods, taking the lead with the same unspoken strength that I've come to rely on. The group starts moving, but it's slow going. The terrain is uneven, and the smoke drifting in makes it hard to see very far down the path.

As we walk, I keep my eyes on the group, especially on a young girl who looks only about sixteen. She's struggling to keep pace, her breaths coming in short gasps.

"Hey," I say, approaching her. "What's your name?"

"Lily," she manages between breaths.

"You doing okay?" I ask, though the answer is clear.

She shakes her head, her eyes wide with fear. "I can't ... I can't breathe," she stutters.

I remember the handkerchief Amber gave me. I untie it from around my neck and hand it to her. "Here, put this over your mouth. It'll help filter the smoke a little."

She nods, tying the cloth around her face. I stay beside her, setting a pace she can keep up with.

The trail winds down the mountain, and with each step, the urgency increases. The smoke thickens, making it hard to see, and the heat from the fire is like a wall pressing against us.

Suddenly, there's a commotion up ahead. Amber has stopped, and the group is bunching up around her. I push my way through to find out what the trouble is.

"What's going on?" I ask.

"There's a fallen tree blocking the path," Amber replies, her voice steady despite the situation. "I'm afraid if we try to go around it, we will find ourselves knee-deep in vegetation and get disoriented. We need to keep on this path."

I look at the obstacle. It's massive. She's right. There's no way around it; we have to go over it.

"Okay, everyone, listen up," I say, raising my voice to be heard over the frightened murmurs of the hikers. "We need to climb over this tree. Be careful, I'll help you."

One by one, they climb over the tree, some with ease, others with difficulty. I help each of them, offering a hand or a boost where needed. When it's Lily's turn, I can see the panic in her eyes.

"You can do this," I reassure her. "I've got you." I stand ready to catch her.

With a trembling nod, she starts to climb. Halfway over, her foot slips, and she lets out a small cry. In an instant, I'm there, steadying her, guiding her over the rest of the way.

Once everyone is safely over, we continue down the trail. The air is hot and thick, stinging my eyes and throat. We're moving as fast as we can, but the fire is all around us.

After what feels like hours, the trail begins to widen. We emerge into a clearing, and for a moment, there's a collective sigh of relief. But it's short-lived.

"That way!" Amber points toward a narrow deer path leading away from the main trail. "It's our best chance."

We don't hesitate, plunging onto the new path. The smoke is less dense here, and I can finally see the sky, a murky orange with the sun struggling to shine through. The wind is blowing the smoke away from us as we create distance from the flames.

As we continue down the trail, the sound of a helicopter can be heard in the distance. Amber leads us to a nearby field where the helicopter lands, its powerful rotor blades kicking up a cloud of dust and debris.

We climb aboard and lift off into the air. The view from above is terrifying, the flames below us seem to stretch on for miles. As we fly away from the fire, I can't help but experience a sense of gratitude mixed with a growing respect for Amber.

Chapter Six

Mark

Once the helicopter touches down and we step out, relief washes over me. We're safe, out of the fire's reach. But as Amber starts talking with the emergency crew who descend upon us, a knot of frustration tightens in my chest.

"Come on. We did our part, Amber," I say, trying to take her hand to steer her away from them. "We got out alive. Why get involved in what happens next? It's not our problem."

She refuses my hand and turns to me. "Not our problem? Mark, this fire could devastate the community, and I'm not going to ignore it."

I can't help but roll my eyes. Her stubbornness is grating on me. "I get that you care about the environment, but this isn't on us. We can't fix everything."

Her expression hardens, and I realize I've hit a sore spot. "You're right, we can't fix everything. But that doesn't mean we shouldn't try," she shoots back. "That's what responsible people do."

"Let the professionals handle it."

"Professionals? We don't have a big fire fancy department here. I'm not walking away from this. I'm a volunteer firefighter, remember? I'm going to do my part, whether you like it or not."

I don't want her in danger. Why can't she see it my way? But her determined look tells me she isn't going to budge.

Just then, a guy pulls up in an SUV, greeting Amber with a hug and a kiss on the cheek. Who is this guy? I wonder, a twinge of jealousy rising.

"Can I drop you off somewhere?" he offers me.

"Mark, this is Ken Ryder," Amber introduces us, and I shake his hand mechanically.

"Our cars are at the trailhead," I say, still processing the sudden appearance of this Ken guy.

During the drive, Ken and Amber talk non-stop about the fire, as if I'm not even there. My plans for a romantic dinner with Amber before I leave dissolve. She's clearly still consumed by the fire.

The car ride feels longer than it is, the silence on my end in stark contrast to their lively conversation. I'm an outsider, and they aren't letting me in. I don't know their relationship, and I'll never find out if I leave.

As we pull up to the trailhead, the reality of my situation starts to sink in. Amber reaches into the back, rummaging through her trunk before appearing with my phone in her hand. "Sorry, I had to lock it in the back during the hike," she explains, handing it over.

I take my phone, but when I press the power button,

nothing happens. The battery is dead. Great. Just great. "Shit," I mutter, pocketing the useless device.

Amber pauses, looking like she wants to say something more, but then she just nods and hops back into her car. "Take care, Mark. It was nice meeting you," she says. And with that, she drives off, leaving me standing there with my pack, a dead phone, and a head full of confusion.

I watch the car disappear, feeling a mix of frustration and disappointment. Here I am, stranded at the trailhead with no way to contact anyone until I can charge my phone. And Amber, the woman who's been part of my life the past few days, is off to fight a fire.

I crawl into my rental car. *Damn it.* I came here for a simple getaway, not to get tangled up in emotions or wildfires. But now, here I am, caught up in both. Amber is different from any woman I've known. She's passionate, determined, and it's clear she's not the type to be swayed from what she believes is right by a guy like me.

I plug my phone into the charger and start driving. I think about my meeting in Texas, the deal that I've been working on for months, waiting for my return.

As I drive, I realize I'm at a crossroads. Part of me wants to chase after Amber, be part of what she's doing, and show her I'm not just some guy who runs away when things get tough. But the other part, the practical, business-minded part, is screaming that I need to get back to Texas, to my life—to what I can control.

I pull into the parking lot of my hotel and go to my room. Stripping out of my hiking gear, I climb into the shower. My mind replays my time in the mountains with Amber. *I've got to let her go. This will never work.*

I dress in tan slacks and a white button-down shirt. I pack my bag. Then sit on the bed with my head in my hands. Despite the thousand reasons I should be figuring out a way to get back to my life in Texas, I'm stuck wondering what my next move should be. Stay or go? Follow my heart or my head? The answers aren't clear, and for the first time in a long time, I feel utterly lost.

Hell, I know this will just complicate things, but I leave my suitcase in my room and race down to my car. I remember Amber mentioning the community center near the base of the mountain.

The moment I drive into the town of Plain, the full extent of the chaos hits me like a physical blow. The street is swarming with emergency vehicles. Firefighters and police officers are everywhere.

I park the car near the Plain Hardware store, where the activity is most concentrated. I spot Amber dressed in her firefighting gear. She's no longer just the woman I was camping with; she's a professional, ready to jump into action.

"Hey, wait up," I call as I run over to join her.

"I need to report in." Her voice is all business, but there's an underlying edge of concern. "There's an emergency volunteer meeting at the community center. I have to go."

I nod. "Of course. Do what you need to do."

She hesitates for a moment, as if she wants to say more, but then disappears into the crowd. I watch her go, feeling a strange mix of pride and worry. She's amazing in her dedication, but the stiffness in her movements tells me this situation is overwhelming even for her.

I should be heading to the airport. My private plane is waiting for me to fly back to Texas. But as I watch the chaos around me and think of Amber diving headfirst into it, something inside me shifts.

I can't leave. Not yet.

Pulling out my phone, I dial my assistant. "Hey, it's Mark. I need to push my trip home a couple of days."

"But, your meeting," she starts to protest.

"I know," I interrupt, my gaze still fixed on the community center where Amber disappeared. "Reschedule it."

As I move through the crowd, I hear snippets of conversation—people worried about their homes, their loved ones, the sheer scope of the disaster. The air is heavy with a mix of fear and determination, a community banding together in the face of adversity.

Amidst it all, I'm out of place, an outsider. This whole situation, the hike, the fire, the chaos, it's thrown me out of balance. It's a foreign concept to me, this idea of community, of shared responsibility. I'm used to being the one in charge. Growing up back in Chicago, if you didn't fight for yourself, no one else would. But here, people fight for each other. And Amber, she's at the heart of it. Her dedication to helping others is awe-inspiring and intimidating.

While I may not be a firefighter or a medical professional, there must be something I can do, some way I can help.

I start walking toward the community center, the decision firm in my mind. I'll find a way to be useful, to contribute. Whatever it is, I need to do something. I can't just sit back and wait while Amber's community faces such a threat.

Inside the community center, the air is thick with a mix of anxiety and purpose. People move about quickly, their faces etched with determination. I take a moment to absorb the scene, the buzz of organized chaos. Volunteers are manning phones, coordinating supplies, and comforting distraught locals.

I approach a woman who seems to be in charge, her hair

pulled back in a no-nonsense ponytail, a walkie-talkie at her hip. "Excuse me," I say. "I'd like to pay for whatever you need."

She stares at me for a moment. "That's generous of you, mister, but that may be beyond your abilities. You have no idea what something like this costs. Besides, we don't know how long this fire will go on. It may be days or months. Go talk to the woman over there. She's in charge of donations." She points to a thin woman with dark hair. Then continues, "We've announced an evacuation in areas that are threatened and got a team going door to door to make sure everyone gets out okay. Most of the hotels are expensive, so there aren't many places for people to stay."

"I can pay for their rooms."

Her eyebrows go up. "That can get quite expensive."

"I can afford it."

"Seriously?" She eyes me with skepticism. "I'll have someone see what's available and have you talk to them, too. But most places will be occupied by tourists right now, so we are directing everyone to come here. If the fire continues, I suspect rooms will open up when the tourists leave, but we just have to deal with what we have now.

I smile. "Is there anything else I can do? My name is Mark Harrison."

She gives me a quick once-over, her expression softening just a touch. "Well, Mark. We need all hands on-deck," she says. "You any good at organizing things?"

"I run a company," I reply. "Organizing is what I do."

"Great." She hands me a clipboard. "We need someone to help coordinate the supply distribution for the emergency shelter. As people arrive, make sure everyone gets what they need—food, water, blankets, that sort of thing. Mostly, they need hope."

I nod, taking the clipboard. "You got it."

She gives me a brief rundown of the system they've set up, then moves on to the next person. I take a deep breath, focusing on the task at hand. It's not my usual boardroom dealings, but it's crucial, lifesaving work.

Standing in the bustling community center, I suddenly feel out of place amidst the displaced locals filtering in. Given the circumstances, my expensive clothes and thousand-dollar cowboy boots seem almost vulgar. These people are losing homes, possessions, and stability.

I listen as the locals start drifting in, displaced by the raging fire threatening their homes. An older woman plops down in a chair near me with exhaustion etched on her face.

"We barely made it out with the clothes on our backs," she says to no one in particular. "Everything I have is in that little house."

A young mother bounces a crying toddler, trying to soothe him. "I know, sweetie, I know. We'll go home soon." But her eyes are filled with uncertainty.

Two teenage boys slump against the wall, headphones still in their ears, stunned looks on their faces. A family of five holds hands with each other, the children's faces stained with tears.

I'm so far removed from the lives of ordinary people, hidden in my sleek high-rise office, making billion-dollar deals, that they feel like foreigners to me. But seeing the very real human impact of this disaster has awakened something in me. I've lived in my bubble for so long—but coming here and meeting Amber has shaken me to my core.

As I stand inside the bustling community center, a young boy sitting alone in a chair catches my eye. Suddenly, I'm taken back to my childhood, struggling to survive. I grew up fast—without the luxury of the small things other kids had. But I snuck into the library and read. It was the only place I could escape into another world.

This kid looks to be about ten years old. In his lap is a book, but he simply stares down at the pages, not reading. His legs kick idly against the chair.

I grab two bottles of water from a nearby table and walk over. "Hi there. Do you mind if I join you for a bit?"

He glances down, taking in my cowboy boots. After a pause, he shrugs.

I offer him a bottle of water and sit on the chair next to him. "I'm Mark. What's your name?"

"Cameron," he says quietly, taking the water.

"What are you reading?" I gesture to the book in his lap. He holds it up—*Harry Potter and the Goblet of Fire*. "I love Harry Potter," I say. "What part are you at?"

"The first task of the Triwizard Tournament. Harry has to get past the dragon." A tiny spark of excitement enters his eyes.

"Oh, that's an intense part! The dragon broke free of its chains, right?" I take a sip of water.

Cameron nods with a sad face. "We left right when I got to that chapter. I wanted to read more, but we had to go ..." His voice trails off. "Uncle Greg and Aunt Mary came over and said it wasn't safe to stay, so we packed up our truck and left. We opened the chicken coop so they could get away first, but I don't think they would know where to go. Daddy took the goats and told Mom he would meet us here after he moved more of our animals. I hope he's okay."

"I know this is really hard," I say gently. "It must be scary not knowing what will happen to your home. But the good news is you have the people out there fighting the fire, your family, and all these here who care about you." The words catch in my throat as it hits me. I remember being a kid and not knowing if I would be safe. The gangs and the gunshots. At least this kid has a safety net.

That brings a small smile to Cameron's face, and I continue, "Maybe we could take turns reading a bit to get your mind off everything for a while?"

Cameron agrees and opens the book. In the crowded, chaotic room, I feel strangely part of something beyond myself. I begin reading, retreating into another world, fighting for what's right.

* * *

Night falls, and the center shows no sign of slowing down. The crisis is ongoing, the fire is still a menacing presence, and from what I hear, they need more people to fight it. I wonder where I can find people to do that. Maybe there are private firefighters I can hire.

I'm checking the latest delivery of supplies when I finally see Amber. She looks exhausted. Our eyes meet across the room, and there's a moment of unspoken understanding. We're both here, doing our part, fighting the same fight.

She makes her way over to me, her steps weary but purposeful. "Hey," she says, her voice hoarse from exertion.

"Hey," I reply, setting down the clipboard. "You okay?"

She nods, a faint smile tugging at her lips. "Yeah. It's been a long day. I didn't expect to see you here."

"I couldn't leave," I admit. "I wanted to be here, for you, for the town."

Her smile grows wider. There is a spark of warmth in her tired eyes. "Thank you, Mark. That means a lot."

We talk briefly about the situation. About the efforts still needed to combat the fire and aid those affected.

As I listen to her, I realize that my decision to stay wasn't just about the crisis. It's about something more, something that's been growing between us since the moment we met. She's already turned my world upside down, and for the first time, I'm not entirely sure what my future holds.

As we part ways, I'm already looking forward to tomorrow, to another day of hard work. This unexpected detour in my life may have started with a hike, but it's leading me down a path I never expected, one that feels surprisingly right.

Chapter Seven

Amber

The following day, I stop by my mom's house to check in on her. The sweet smell of my mom's famous chocolate chip cookies makes my mouth water when I enter the kitchen. She's busy bagging up dozens of them for the firefighters battling the blaze.

"Hey, Mom," I say, giving her a hug. "How's it going?"

"Oh, just trying to do my part to keep spirits up," she replies. "I canceled all the B&B reservations since no tourist in their right mind would vacation here right now. But I've opened up the rooms for any locals who are displaced. Hopefully, these cookies will give the firefighters a little pick-me-up too."

Leave it to my mom to be thinking of everyone else, even in a crisis. Before I can respond, the back door bangs open and in tromp my brothers Grady and Matt. As adults, they still behave like rambunctious teenagers whenever they're together. A moment later, my other brother Chris shows up.

"What's the latest on the fire?" Grady asks, putting his arm around my shoulder.

I unlock my phone and pull up the app with updates. They gather around as I show them the latest briefing for the fire crew. The blaze has spread faster than anticipated, thanks to the winds picking up. Containment is still maybe a week out, even in the best-case scenario. Wildland firefighters are coming in from other parts of the country to help.

Grady swears under his breath. His house is one of those under a Level 2 evacuation order. Matt claps a sympathetic hand on his shoulder. "We'll go up and hose things down, just in case any embers make it that far," he says.

"Thank God the winery is on the other side of town," Mom smiles at Chris.

"Count me in on helping you save your house, bro." Chris nods. "I've other people covering for me right now. Family is more important than selling a few bottles of wine."

I frown, worry furrowing my brow. "If this wind keeps up, that area will be a Level 3 before you know it. I don't think that's a good idea ..." I begin but trail off after seeing the stubborn set of Grady's jaw. There'll be no talking my brothers out of this. "At least check on the neighbors if you go," I concede. "Make sure no one is still there who shouldn't be."

My mom pinches her eyebrows together, casting a worried look at my brother. "Grady, promise me you and your brothers won't take any unnecessary risks," she begs.

"We'll be careful, Mom," he reassures her, though we all know 'careful' is not a word commonly associated with Grady.

"You know I have the guest house out back. Why don't you plan to stay there tonight, just to be safe, Grady," Jess suggests.

"I don't want to worry about you staying up there tonight." Jess rubs Grady's arm. "Please."

I can see she's already shaken by the idea of him heading up to his house—their future house.

"Yeah, I think that's best. I don't want to have to send someone up there to drag your ass back if you had any thoughts about staying to face the flames. We need all the help on the line right now, not chasing down idiots like you."

Grady scratches his stubbled cheek, considering. Then glances at Jess, whose eyes are full of worry. "Yeah, all right," he finally agrees.

"Promise?"

"Yes, I promise."

Jess gives him a hug and a kiss.

Relieved, my mom sighs. She begins packing up cookies for Grady, Matt, and Chris to take with them. Matt grabs one to munch on as he heads for the door. Some things never change.

I give Grady one last look. "Seriously, be smart," I tell him. "And call if you are in trouble."

He grins and ruffles my hair like he used to do when we were kids, knowing it annoys me. "Yes, little firefighter."

I swat his hand away, which only makes him laugh as he follows Matt out. The door bangs shut behind them, and the kitchen feels strangely quiet. My mom and I look at each other. I know we're both worried about my brothers heading closer to the danger, but also confident they can handle themselves.

I linger in the kitchen, reluctant to leave my mom despite my responsibilities calling me elsewhere.

"How are you holding up, really?" I ask her, watching her face tense as she scoops cookie dough onto the baking sheets.

She pauses, glancing up at me. "Oh, you know me. I just need to keep busy."

It's her coping mechanism—the more anxious she feels, the more furiously she'll work—but I also see the strain around her eyes that gives away her worry for all of us.

"They'll be okay," I say in an effort to reassure both of us. "They may be thickheaded, but they know when to be careful."

Mom nods before changing the subject. "Did you manage to convince more people to evacuate the area?"

As a volunteer firefighter, I've been helping to alert civilians in high-risk zones. Most people heed the warnings once they see the growing smoke plumes and falling ash. But there are always holdouts stubbornly convinced it won't impact them.

"A few more," I reply. "Old Joe Keller still refuses to budge, though. If those boys drive up that way, maybe they can talk some sense into him when they check the area."

I glance out the window as a convoy of cars comes up the driveway to the B&B. There must be half a dozen of them packed full of families and their belongings. My heart twists for them as they spill out onto the gravel, faces weary and streaked with ash.

A harried mom holding a baby sees me peering out and makes her way over. "I'm so sorry to just show up like this," she says breathlessly. "But we didn't know where else to go. Our neighborhood got the evacuation notice, but many hotels are full already."

"Of course, I understand completely," Mom assures her. "I've opened the B&B rooms for anyone displaced by the fires. Let's get you and your family settled."

I usher her inside and do a quick count. "Mom. There's more coming."

She smiles as they come through the door. "It looks like I have enough rooms for all of you if some families don't mind sharing." A relieved sigh ripples through the group. Jess passes out keys, and I recognize a few of my mom's friends from around town. They share tearful hugs and a few encouraging words before Jess shows them upstairs.

My heart breaks for all of them. In one awful instant, normal life has been ruthlessly interrupted and replaced by this smoky chaos.

I rush outside to find more familiar faces. The Henderson boys climb out, faces streaked with soot. "Sorry, Ms. Holloway," the older one mumbles. "Our place got torched bad. We got the horses out, but that's it. Took them down in the valley to the Willow's farm."

As I lead them inside, I swear to myself that I will do everything possible to stop this fire from ruining more lives.

I peer out the window again, where the daylight has taken on an unearthly orange-gray hue from the smoke haze. Ash flakes drift in the air like sinister snowflakes. It reminds me I can't linger here.

"I should get back to the fire station," I say reluctantly. "Chief wants us out checking on places to make sure people have left."

Mom halts her bustling to give me a fierce hug. "You stay safe out there, too," she admonishes. "No risky business. Don't spread yourself too thin, sweetheart."

I smile against her hair. "Look who's talking. I swear you and Grady are more alike than you think."

She swats me playfully with a dish towel as I dodge away, laughter breaking the tension. But I know she'll keep a bag packed just in case she, too, gets an evacuation notice. My strong-willed mother doesn't scare easily, although having kids heading into disaster areas isn't helping her peace of mind.

Settling behind the wheel, I close my watery eyes. There

will be time later for looking back and counting our blessings. For now, duty demands focusing forward, using my training to serve my community alongside my firefighting family. As I head out, I glance back and see her silhouette in the window, her shoulders bowed under an invisible weight.

My phone rings as I'm driving to the fire station. I don't recognize the number flashing on my screen. Normally, I'd let an unknown caller go to voicemail, but it could be important with everything that's happening.

I put it on speaker. "Hello?"

"Amber! Oh my god, I just saw the news about the wildfire back home. Are you okay?" My sister Kim's worried voice floods through the phone.

I guess no one had called Kim to let her know. She's away on her honeymoon in Hawaii with her new husband, Ethan. With everything going on, I know I'd forgotten.

"Yeah, I'm fine," I assure her. "I'm headed back to the fire station now. We're still trying to contain the blaze."

"How close is it to town?" I can hear the edge of panic in her voice.

"It's miles out still. Don't worry, your place is safe along with mom's B&B." I hesitate before adding, "It is getting close to Grady's, though. He, Matt, and Chris just headed up there to hose things down."

Kim sucks in a sharp breath. "Those idiots! Why would they go toward the fire?"

Despite everything, I chuckle. It's such a Kim response. "You know how they are. But please don't cut the honeymoon short—we've got things under control here. So, don't worry."

Kim pauses. "Hey, is Mark still there?"

I sigh at the mention of Mark. "Yeah, he's been great," I say, hoping I sound casual rather than conflicted. "He stepped up to organize a lot of relief."

Kim adds. "Ethan says he's a great guy. It would be wonderful if you two ended up together."

I bite my lip, gazing on the road ahead. "I don't know Kimmy," I tell her. "This isn't really the time to think about dating. We're just focused on getting through this fire first."

It's not a firm rejection, but I hope she gets the hint to let it go without turning it into a big thing. I have enough complications to handle with an out-of-control wildfire raging nearby without adding possible romance into the mix.

Chapter Eight

Amber

The forest is dense, a tall green shroud that muffles the world outside. I navigate the narrow, unkempt path in the fire department's rugged SUV, the scent of pine and earth heavy in the air. I'm alone on this road today, tasked with a final sweep through the cabins to ensure everyone's evacuated before the fire spreads.

As I pull up to the first cabin, the engine's rumble seems louder in the heavy silence. I note the deserted front yard—no vehicles, and outdoor furniture is stacked haphazardly near the porch. "Anyone home?" I call out, peering through the windows.

I get no response. The interior seems to be empty as well. I'm relieved to find another family safely evacuated.

I hop back in my vehicle and continue on, weaving slowly between the tall pines. At each cabin, I follow the same routine

—looking for signs of anyone still home, checking out the interior and reporting my findings over the crackling radio. "Another cabin clear," I confirm.

Most are already vacant, with personal items and vehicles conspicuously absent. Some show signs of rushed evacuation —a pile of clothes left on a bed, dirty dishes in a sink.

The smoky scent grows stronger now, tendrils creeping through the lush pine. My stomach tightens each time I press the radio to my ear, hoping for an update from my supervisor on the fire's progress. The responses are still pretty much the same—it keeps spreading because of the wind and dry conditions, but it's tough to say how fast because of the dense forest. Still, I'm told to hurry. We need to confirm complete evacuation before the flames close in.

I reach another small cabin tucked deeper into the woods than the rest. The cracked driveway is empty, and the dilapidated porch sits without furniture. "Fire department, anyone still on the property?" Peering into the grime-coated window reveals a humble interior—outdated appliances and nondescript furniture. It's classic rental cabin décor. I try the front door, more out of due diligence than suspicion. The knob turns easily, and the door creaks open. Dust motes catch the sunlight streaming through windows. Silence, stillness, emptiness. From the looks of things, it's been vacant for some time. I close the door, get back into my SUV, and head out to the next place.

As I pull around toward the cabin's rear, a sense of unease creeps over me. The surrounding forest seems darker, dense pines replacing sun-dappled aspens. The smoky scent clings heavier here. I kill the engine and step out, my boots sinking slightly into the soft, damp soil. I sweep my flashlight in arcs, shadows dancing across the mossy stone and timber. Is that fire

I smell or just smoke on the wind? I worry about my brothers. My radio check-in reveals no alarming updates—the fire continues its creeping spread. Still, no new evacuation orders have been called in Grady's area.

I circle the weed-choked yard, my gaze darting about for anything amiss. As I reach the back porch, ready to report my unremarkable findings, I hear a soft whimpering, barely audible over the rustling leaves. My heart tightens. Was some small woodland creature hiding? No. This sounds more canine. I sweep my light under the porch. Two glinting eyes reflect back. I jerk in surprise before recognizing the shivering form—a dog!

I scan the yard and surrounding forest again. Still no signs of inhabitants—no vehicle, no tire tracks that aren't my own, no footprints in the muddy soil. Just me and this poor abandoned mut.

"Oh no," I whisper. "Who left you out here?"

Heart pounding, I crouch down, one hand still gripping my radio. "Hey there," I whisper.

I slowly extend my free hand, keeping my movements smooth and my voice low. "Come on out. I won't hurt you."

The dog stares back, eyes blinking against the flashlight beam, brown and white fur quivering. It's some kind of spaniel mix, hardly twenty pounds. Its slender frame suggests some neglect. But the eyes are still soft, round, trusting. This one seems accustomed to humans, not feral. How long has it been hiding under here, I wonder?

"It's ok, I'm here to help," I murmur. The dog shuffles back slightly with a faint whine. Scared and starving, I guess. But also, not aggressive. I ease myself to the damp soil, heedless of my uniform, angling the flashlight to avoid the direct glare. The dog watches me, nose twitching, ears shifting. I hold my hand steady, breathing slowly, keeping my movements minimal. The last thing I want is to startle the poor thing into bolting off into the woods.

After an endless moment, the dog stretches its neck slowly forward. I feel the warm tickle of its breath as it catches my scent. My fingers tremble slightly as I maintain my pose. Then, contact. The brush of a cold, damp nose against my fingertips. Success! Slowly, murmuring praise and comfort, I ease closer until I can stroke the dog's matted fur. Matted but not visibly marred by injuries—another sign it's used to human interaction.

As I caress its back with long, smooth strokes, the dog leans into my touch, tail giving the slightest wag. Poor thing is starving for affection.

Once the dog seems soothed enough by my touch, I broadcast a report over the radio: "This is Amber Holloway. I've located an abandoned dog at cabin eight; no other signs of inhabitants. Requesting animal pickup at checkpoint rendezvous."

My supervisor's static response affirms the procedure, "An animal control trailer will meet you at the checkpoint to transport the dog to safety."

Signing off, I shift my focus to the wide, soulful eyes peering up at me.

I ease a hand under the dog's belly, speaking soothing encouragement. It stiffens slightly but allows my encircling grip. I draw it gently from its dark sanctuary into the afternoon sunlight. The dog moves easily, legs and paws shifting automatically to aid me rather than resist.

I cradle the shivering bundle in my arms, holding it close to my chest. My assessment is correct. It's a female, mid-sized, underweight. But after a full minute of my cradling embrace, her trembling softens to occasional twitches. She is as cute as can be with a pink and black two-tone nose and one ear lopsided.

I place the dog gently on the passenger seat of my SUV. She sniffs around before nestling into my discarded jacket, head resting on folded paws. I run my palm over the soft fur of her back before closing the door.

In my driver's seat once more, I lower the windows halfway. The scent of wood smoke permeates the cab. As I leave, the emergency radio buzzes. I quickly activate it to hear the latest fire update.

The fire continues to spread faster than predicted. The nearest edge only two miles from my current location. Containment lines are still distant. Gusting winds are driving the flames erratically. I grip the wheel tighter, my urgency heightening. Checkpoint rendezvous in ten minutes.

My gaze flicks to the dog. She meets my eyes, then snuggles back into my jacket.

I proceed steadily through the forest, retracing the routes between marked cabins. All are still deserted, my thorough sweeps confirmed.

Five minutes now til rendezvous. The smoke scent strengthens, mingling with the hints of actual burning nearby. The air warms against my face despite the chilly breeze through the windows. My dog companion lifts her head with a muted whine. She smells it, too. I stroke a hand along her side in reassurance as I steer us closer to safety. She licks my fingertips in response, then lays her speckled head in my lap.

I pull into the checkpoint station—once a cheery ranger welcome site, now converted to a smoke-veiled command center bustling with emergency vehicles and personnel. The promised animal control trailer sits off to the side. I bring my

SUV alongside, get out, and gently lift my precious cargo. Her warmth seeps into my skin as she snuggles close, trusting and calm despite the shouts, engine rumbles, and smoke stinging the air.

Two wildlife technicians stand ready by the trailer. I reluctantly transfer the dog to their waiting gloves. She resists only a moment, nails scrabbling against my jacket. "It's ok sweetheart, you'll be safe. Good girl," I say to her.

A volunteer steps closer, logging down details and statistics—where and when found, approximate breed, gender, age—all crucial identifiers should an owner come seeking their lost pet.

Once logged, the technicians secure the dog safely into a transport cage. She watches me through the metal grid door. I crouch to her level once more, fingers instinctively reaching. She licks my hand in response, then lays her head atop her folded paws.

One technician clasps my shoulder, reminding me gently to move along. My duty done, I must make way for the next arrival.

I let out a sigh and say goodbye. "It's okay. We'll find your owner or someone to take care of you."

I climb into my vehicle and adrenaline floods my senses once more. No longer alone on this assignment, two trucks now follow as reinforcement support. Twice we come upon vehicles, with people standing around who've called for help. My companions help transport the grateful but terrified families to safety.

In the distance, we can see that flames have consumed the forest we patrolled just hours ago. Over the radio, we receive orders to turn our convoy toward the station and head home.

* * *

I arrive at my cabin to find several dozen bouquets of pink roses on my doorstep. I don't need to guess who they are from. I take the flowers inside, cut them down, and put them in mason jars to set around the room. It's a sweet gesture from Mark and just the thing to lift my spirits.

Chapter Nine

Mark

I knock on the door of Amber's cabin, balancing bags of takeout food in one hand.

"It's open!" Amber's voice calls from within.

I nudge the door open with my foot and step inside. Amber is in the bathroom, scrubbing the soot and dirt from her face with a washcloth.

"I come bearing food," I announce, holding up the takeout bags.

"Thanks, Mark. And thanks for the lovely flowers. That's very nice of you." She smiles then turns. "I think I need a quick shower. I'll be out in a few minutes."

"Sure. I'll put the bags in the kitchen." Around the tiny living room are the roses I sent sticking out of little mason jars and candles burning. A carved bear and a bowl of pinecones are on the coffee table. I smile. Amber's place seems primitive compared to my lavish modern condo. Not that I spend much time there. I'm usually jet-setting between my various hotels and resort locations.

I hear the shower water running, wondering what Amber looks like with the hot water and steam surrounding her. I smile at the thought.

Amber appears, wearing leggings and an oversized sweatshirt with a Seahawks logo on the front, her hair still damp. She breaks into a tired yawn. "You are a lifesaver. I'm absolutely ravenous," she says, while inhaling deeply. "Mmm, Italian food. My favorite."

Amber grabs some plates while I open a bottle of Chianti.

"This was so thoughtful of you," she says, grinning. "It's just what I needed after an endless day."

I get that familiar warmth seeing her smile. "It was the least I could do. You've all been working all day."

Over dinner, Amber tells me stories about her day and rescuing the puppy. Her eyes light up, and I can tell she wanted to bring the dog home with her, but knew it belonged to someone else.

After we finish eating, Amber settles onto the sofa, looking exhausted. I busy myself rinsing the dishes in the sink. When I return, she's fast asleep with her head slumped onto a pillow.

I pause, studying her as she breathes deeply. An affectionate warmth blooms inside me. Careful not to wake her, I lift Amber's feet and gently swing them onto the couch. I drape a woven blanket lightly over her sleeping form.

She looks so peaceful that I can't bring myself to leave just yet. Instead, I settle into an armchair nearby and watch the light from the candles dance over her face. For once, my mind isn't racing; I'm feeling content here in this cabin in the woods with her.

I think about my world back in the city—skyscrapers, boardrooms, the constant hum of ambition. It's a world where success is measured in contracts and concrete. Yet, here, in this simple, candlelit room, I find a different kind of success. It's in the quiet, the stillness, the way Amber's presence seems to make time slow down.

I've always prided myself on being decisive, knowing what I want. But Amber, she's different. She challenges my perceptions and makes me question what I truly value. As a property developer, I've reshaped city skylines, turning visions into steel and glass realities. But Amber, she reshapes lives, touches hearts. She's not just a gift shop owner or a volunteer firefighter; she's a pillar of this community, a beacon of warmth and generosity.

And here I am, a man who thought he had life figured out, suddenly unsure of everything except for the feeling stirring in my chest. It's a vulnerability I've spent years burying myself under contracts and blueprints. A feeling that terrifies me because it doesn't fit into any of my plans. Yet, as I sit here, watching her sleep, I realize that maybe, just maybe, the best things in life aren't planned. They're felt, experienced, in times like these, where the world outside doesn't matter. All that exists is the present moment, the soft glow of candlelight, and the dawning awareness that I am irrevocably drawn to this remarkable woman.

A sudden whimper from Amber jolts me from my thoughts. Her face contorts in distress, and she thrashes under the blanket. "No, Derek!" she cries out.

I quickly kneel by her side, gripping her shoulder. "Amber, wake up," I urge. "You're having a bad dream."

With a shuddering gasp, her eyes fly open, brimming with

tears. She takes a few seconds to get her bearings. "Mark?" she whispers. "What are you doing here?"

"You fell asleep after dinner. I didn't want to leave you alone."

She slowly sits up, rubbing her eyes. "I'm sorry you had to see that. The nightmare ... it's always the same."

My chest aches to see her so shaken. I sit down beside her. "What were you dreaming about?" I ask.

Amber stares down at her lap, rubbing the blanket between her fingers. "Fire," she murmurs.

"Maybe you shouldn't be out there if it's seeping into your dreams."

She draws a shaky breath before continuing softly. "No, this is about a different fire. It's always about Derek, my ex-fiancé. We lived in an old farmhouse together. It had faulty wiring that sparked a fire and ..."

Her voice catches. She shakes her head, not wanting to recall the memory, but does. "I escaped out the door when the smoke alarm sounded. But Derek was upstairs gathering his computer and files. The flames spread so fast ... there was no way for him to get out."

My heart constricts hearing her anguish. I wrap an arm around her shoulder. To my relief, she leans into me.

"I freaked out. I called 9-1-1, but I had to stand there, help-less, as the entire house burned with Derek trapped inside." She squeezes her eyes shut. "By the time the firefighters arrived, it was too late. He didn't make it."

I feel like I've been punched in the gut as Amber describes her recurring nightmare. The raw anguish in her voice is heart-wrenching. Tightening my arm around her shoulders, I wish I could somehow absorb her pain.

"I still have nightmares about it," she admits wearily. "I'm standing outside the burning house, hearing Derek scream my name over and over. I tried to run in to save him but couldn't get close because of the flames and intense smoke. I didn't know what to do, so I ran back outside. Then I heard that awful crashing sound as the roof caved in. Then his screaming stopped."

She shudders, fresh tears welling up in her eyes. "And I have to live with the guilt that I escaped, and he didn't. That I couldn't save the man I loved more than anything."

She clings to me as sobs overtake her slender frame. I rub her back, murmuring soft, meaningless words of comfort.

At last, her tears quit flowing. Utterly spent, she slumps against my chest. I continue holding her close, trying to surround her with a sense of peace and safety, to chase away the haunting memories, if only for a moment.

"I'm so sorry you had to go through something so horrible," I say gently. "But please believe me, his death was absolutely not your fault. You did everything you could. You can't blame yourself for a tragic accident beyond your control."

She nods slightly against my chest, but I can tell the guilt still weighs heavily on her. We sit in silence as I smooth back her hair, keeping her cradled close. "I'm so sorry, Amber," I say, finding my throat tight. "I can't imagine how painful that was."

She nods against my shoulder. "It's why I became a volunteer firefighter. If I can help just one person escape that agony ..." she trails off, taking a deep breath.

I grasp her hand. "Derek would be proud of you for using his tragedy to help others."

Amber lifts her head. "You really think so?"

"I know so. You're the most compassionate, courageous person I've ever met." I tenderly tuck back her hair.

She smiles. "That means a lot coming from you."

I chuckle. "Yeah. Well, I'm not as impressive as people think." My tone turns serious. "But you truly are impressive, Amber. Never doubt that."

Her smile widens, and she wraps both arms around me in a fierce hug.

"Thank you, Mark," she whispers.

I close my eyes, holding Amber close to me. "Anytime," I murmur into her hair.

We stay that way for a long moment, taking comfort in each other's embrace. For several heartbeats, I allow myself to get lost in the feeling of Amber in my arms—her warm embrace, her silky hair against my cheek.

Slowly, I loosen my hold to meet her gaze. Amber's eyes are still rimmed in red, but the anguish has faded, replaced by a soft vulnerability that makes my chest ache.

Unable to resist, I gently brush my thumb over her cheek, wiping away the last of her tear's wetness. Amber draws in a shaky breath but doesn't pull away.

Emboldened, I begin to slowly lean in, cradling her jaw. Giving her time to protest. But she remains still, her lips parting slightly as her eyes close.

My cell phone shatters the silence. I freeze. Then exhale heavily, dropping my forehead to rest against Amber's.

"I should get this. It could be important," I say reluctantly.

Amber nods, avoiding my gaze. Her cheeks are tinged pink. "Of course."

She busies herself while I step outside. I listen to the message, asking when I'm returning. Cursing under my breath, I silence my phone.

I grip the porch railing, reality hitting me. What am I doing? I need to go back to Texas. I can't get involved with

Amber. Yes, I'm drawn to her dedication, her passion. But relationships aren't my thing. My world is business deals and profits, not intimacy and emotions.

If we continue this, I'll only end up hurting her when my shortcomings become clear. Or when she realizes how damaged I am once my glossy veneer fades.

Better to leave things as they are. I should go back to Texas and let her move on. It's the sensible choice. The safe one. Isn't it?

I head back inside. Amber's rinsing wine glasses, her back to me.

"Everything okay at the office?" she asks lightly.

"Yeah, nothing urgent." I hover in the doorway, hands in my pockets.

"Well, it's getting late ..." Her voice trails off as she turns to face me, uncertainty etched on her delicate features.

I swallow back the ache in my throat. "I should let you rest," I manage to say.

Unable to stop myself, I gently kiss her forehead. "Goodnight, Amber," I whisper. Then I slip out before she can respond, the faint scent of smoke and vanilla lingering as I walk back alone. I still can't let go of the certainty that I don't deserve her. That I have nothing *real* to offer this woman, only superfluous tokens of my success.

Chapter Ten

Amber

I gaze across the water between healthy trees. An eerie orange glow covers the sky. Miniscule particles fill the air. In the distance, tiny flares dot the forest like intermittent breaths exhaled by an angry dragon.

As our truck travels closer, there is something mesmerizing about the dancing flames and their reflections across the lake's glassy surface.

Along the hillside are smoldering skeletons of blackened trees outlined by an otherworldly light. Tendrils of lingering smoke curl around the base of the trees like a surreal serpent. The contrast is both frightening and oddly beautiful at the same time.

I know this is nature's way of purging the layers of underbrush and unwanted growth. But like floods, rockslides, and other dramatic acts of devastation, regardless of what we do, there will be an impact on people's lives. Our job today is to stop this hungry monster from creeping closer, devouring more homes. With our Pulaski axes, hoes, and shovels, we will cut vegetation and manage a small burn line, while the swampers clear a path with heavy equipment and plows hoping to detour the inferno.

* * *

The moment I return to civilization, my body screams for rest. The fire, relentless and unforgiving, has drained every ounce of energy from my bones. My eyes are bloodshot from the smoke, my muscles ache from the exertion of cutting brush. After two straight days in the forest, each step back to the station feels heavier than the last.

Shedding my soot-stained suit, I take a moment to breathe and regroup. My limbs are like jelly, and my throat is raw and dry from yelling orders over the noise of the chainsaws. I dig deep for the strength to make one last stop before I can collapse at home. I promised Mom I would check in if I got a chance.

At the community center, I can see she's busy organizing clothes and toiletries for the families who had to evacuate their homes. She spots me in the doorway and relief floods her face.

"Hi, sweetheart, you look dead on your feet. When's the last time you ate a decent meal?"

I wave off her fussing, too exhausted for mothering right now.

"I'm fine, Mom. Just wanted to let you know I'm headed home to crash. You seem to have everything under control here."

Her eyebrows knit together as she looks me up and down, maternal concern all over her face. She knows I'm running on borrowed energy, but also knows not to push me when I'm like this.

"Well, I'm worried about you exhausting yourself. At least let me bring over a casserole later for you to eat."

"No, don't worry about me. You have your hands full here and at the B&B with all the evacuees. I can take care of myself."

I can tell she's itching to override my refusal and force me to rest, but she simply squeezes my arm and sighs.

"Okay, if you insist. But call me later so I know you're all right?"

"I will. Thanks, Mom." I give her a tired smile, and she pulls me in for a quick but tight hug.

As I head for the door, I feel her watching me, longing to make everything okay, even in the midst of this crisis. But for now, all I can manage is to put one foot in front of the other until I reach my bed.

As I trudge back through the parking lot, I notice the media has descended upon the area. Cameras, microphones, reporters—it's not surprising, given the severity of the fires. These kinds of disasters always draw attention. But what catches my eye is Mark, surrounded by a swarm of reporters. They're hanging on his every word while cameras are rolling.

I overhear him talking about his financial donations to the rescue efforts, his voice carrying over the crowd. I can't help but feel a twinge of cynicism. It all seems too polished, too perfect. There he is, the successful businessman, playing the part of the generous benefactor. I watch as he answers questions. His demeanor is friendly, even charming.

It's all a show, isn't it? A publicity stunt? He's just like every other rich guy out there, using a crisis to boost his own image. I can't stand the thought of it. The way he seems to bask in the attention and how the media eats it up.

Feeling a mix of exhaustion and disillusionment, I turn away. I don't want to be part of that spectacle. I've been fighting an actual battle out there, not playing hero for the cameras. The thought of Mark being part of this media circus and exploiting this disaster for his own gain makes my stomach turn.

Wanting to put as much distance between myself and that scene as possible, I pick up my pace. I thought Mark was different, wanting to believe there was something genuine about him. But seeing him there, in the middle of all that attention, is a reminder of the world of the wealthy, where appearances matter more than actions, where gestures are often hollow. The idea saddens me more than I want to admit.

The town around me is still buzzing with activity. But at this moment, I'm more alone than ever. It's a familiar feeling that I've tried to outrun, to bury under my dedication to my work and my community. I don't want to feel heartbreak ever again.

I can't call my sister to process my feelings because she's off on her honeymoon and needs to focus on her happiness, not my problems. I straighten up, pushing the disappointment to the back of my mind. I have work to do, and people to help. I can't get caught up in whatever game Mark is playing. There are bigger things at stake, real lives affected by this tragedy.

A sharp reminder pricks at my consciousness. I need to eat something. The thought almost escaped me amidst the turmoil of the day and the jumble of emotions swirling inside. I'm confused. My blood sugar has dropped, reminding me of my vulnerability and that I need to take care of myself.

Opening the door to my SUV, I slide behind the wheel. Pawing through the glove box I take out some dried fruit. I chew slowly. Then I down it with water from the extra bottle that I always keep under the seat. Feeling slightly better, I start up my car.

The drive home feels mechanical, my mind still wrestling with the events of the day—the fire, the media, and Mark.

Pulling into my driveway, the familiar sight of my home offers little comfort. It's a refuge, but tonight, it feels more like a place to collapse. As I turn off the engine and gather my strength to get out, the sharp sound of my cell phone cuts through the car's silence.

Mark

Seeing his name flash on the screen sends a jolt through me, a mix of anticipation and irritation. I hesitate, my finger hovering over the phone. I let the call go to voicemail.

Inside my house, I'm too tired to cook and opt for a microwaved dinner. I chow down, hardly tasting the food. The day has left me drained, not just physically but emotionally, too. The fire, the adrenaline, and now this confusion over Mark—it's all too much.

After eating, I barely have the energy to clean up. I leave the dishes in the sink. My bed beckons, and I can't reach it fast enough.

As I drop into bed, my body sinks into the mattress, a deep, almost desperate tiredness enveloping me. But even as my eyes close, my mind refuses to shut off. Images flash behind my eyelids—flames, smoke, Mark's face, his voice.

* * *

The pounding on my door jolts me awake. I sit up with a start, momentarily disoriented. Rubbing sleep from my eyes, I glance at the clock: it's 10:00 a.m. I slip on my robe and shuffle toward the door, my body still heavy with exhaustion. Yesterday was such a long, draining day that I'm still feeling its effects.

Opening the door cautiously, I'm met with the last person I expected to see—Mark. He's standing there on my doorstep, wearing dark jeans and a light blue button-down shirt, with a look of concern across his handsome face.

"Amber, I've been worried sick about you," he says. "When I didn't hear from you yesterday ... Are you okay?"

"Yeah," I reply, tying the belt to my robe tighter. "What's up?"

He smiles. "If you have the day off, I thought we could spend it together."

Spend the day with him? I yawn. His suggestion sounds interesting, but then the image of him with the press flashes in my mind. I pinch my eyebrows together and bark at him, "What the hell were you doing talking to the press yesterday? Did you call a press conference?" I can't keep the accusation from my voice. "From the sound of it, you were single-handedly rescuing the town."

"No, you've got that wrong," he explains, holding up his hands defensively. "The press got wind that I was in town and made a big deal out of it."

I throw my hair over my shoulder. "Why are you still here? You got your photo op," I cut in, my frustration rising. "Don't you need to rush back to your important life and career?"

Mark's expression shifts—a mix of frustration and something else—disappointment, maybe?

He takes a deep breath. "I stayed because I was worried. The money I donated wasn't for show. I want to help, that's all."

"Is that so?"

He nods, holding my gaze with his piercing hazel eyes through the clump of hair that has fallen forward.

"Yes, it's true, I promise. It might be hard to believe I would do such a thing. But I'm not heartless."

I want to believe him, but I'm wary of being fooled. Men like him only do things that benefit themselves. Didn't he tell me in the mountains that he believed everyone was only in it for themselves?

"Look, Mark," I say, choosing my words carefully. "I appreciate your coming by and your concern. But I'm not sure what to think right now. Yesterday was ... a lot. And seeing you with the press after spending all day on the lines. It just ..." I trail off, unsure how to express the turmoil inside me.

I can see the worry creasing on his brow.

He reaches out and touches my arm with his hand. "Don't dismiss me. Please. I wouldn't be here if I didn't care about you. I should be in Texas right now, but I'm not."

"So, you will still be leaving soon?"

He looks at me. "I ... do have a company to run that I'll have to get back to."

"Just go then. Leave."

He touches my face. "Amber, I know this isn't what you want to hear. But I can come back."

"When?"

He drops his hand. "I don't know. I'll just have to shuffle my schedule around. Maybe we can meet somewhere. I can fly you to ..."

"No. This isn't going to work."

He pulls me to him and looks down at me. "I'm not giving up on you."

My lips tremble.

He kisses me, and I fall apart. Tears stream down my eyes.

Damn him. Our kisses get deeper, and he picks me up and pushes the door open and carries me inside, then sets me on the couch.

He kisses my neck, and all I can think of is how much I want to be held by him. All my stress bursts through, and I fall apart. He holds me tight, then strokes my hair as I sob.

"It's okay. Let it all out," he whispers. "I'm here for you."

Once I quit crying, he hands me a kerchief from his pocket. I dab my eyes. Then try to smile. "I'm sorry."

"Hush, there is nothing to be sorry about. You must be exhausted."

I nod my head.

"I'm worried that you are pushing yourself too hard. Other people are fighting this fire, too. You don't have to take this on as your personal responsibility. I've let it be known the community needs help. I talked with the man in charge, and firefighters are coming in from other parts of the country to help."

"I have to. It's important to me."

Mark sits back down on the couch beside me. "I get that. But you need to take better care of yourself."

I bite my lower lip. "I know," I say defensively.

Mark reaches over and takes my hand in his. "I don't want to lose you."

"When are you leaving?"

"Tomorrow."

"Oh. When are you coming back?"

"It depends. I've got an important deal I'm working on. I'll call and let you know."

"Right. This is just what I don't want."

"Hey, I promise I'll be back as quick as I can."

"I appreciate you coming by, but I need some time to catch up on things and rest."

"Sure. I'll let you be. I'll call you while I'm gone." He stares at me. "Can I kiss you goodbye?"

I nod, and he takes me in his arms. We kiss, and I don't want him to leave. But I break it off. "Go," I tell him, pushing him away, then wiping my tears.

After I close the door, my vision starts to blur around the edges, a sure sign my glucose has dipped dangerously low. I make my way shakily to the kitchen to grab some juice and make myself a peanut butter sandwich. I wolf it down. As I begin to feel better, Mark's actions replay in my mind. Knowing he cares about the town and me is comforting, despite my apprehension.

The phone rings. Seeing it's Mom calling, I answer, a slight sense of relief washing over me. Her voice, always a mix of concern and comfort, is a welcome intrusion.

"Hi, honey. I just wanted to check on you, make sure you aren't pushing yourself too hard," she says, her tone laced with motherly worry.

"Thanks, Mom," I respond, trying to sound more upbeat than I feel.

"I know you want to help the community, but you need to take care of yourself, too. Are you eating right and watching your blood sugar?" she asks, her voice firm, reminding me of the countless times she's been my unwavering support.

"Yeah," I tell her, though the truth is, today, I'm completely wiped. The past day's events, physical demands, and emotional turmoil have left me drained.

"That's good, honey."

There's a pause, and I can picture Mom, on the other end of the line mixing up a bowl of cookies in her kitchen.

"Just promise me you'll be careful, Amber. And take a

break if you need to. You're no good to anyone if you burn out."

Her words resonate with me. "I promise, Mom," I reply. Though I know it's hard to step back and not throw myself completely into the situation.

"Grady is still worried about his house, but Jess has persuaded him not to go there again."

"Tell him he can build another house."

"You know your brother. But you are right. He's got the finances to start over. Not like some of the other people around here."

"How are you doing with all those people at the B&B?"

"You know what they say about too many cooks. Everyone is trying their best not to be a burden, but I don't like strangers in my kitchen."

"How's Jess doing?"

"She is a godsend. I'm so glad I hired her. She's so organized. Taking the burden off my shoulders so I can escape to work at the community center for a few hours."

"That's good," I tell her.

"And how are things otherwise? Is everything okay? Did you enjoy your hike?" she asks, her voice hinting at more than just my physical well-being.

I hesitate. The image of Mark at my door flashes in my mind. Do I tell her? Share the confusion? The unexpected twist in my life?

"It's ... complicated," I finally say, opting for honesty. "There's a lot going on right now."

Mom's always had a sixth sense about these things. "Is this about that man you mentioned? Ethan's friend. Mark, is it?"

"Yes."

"I've heard he's done a great job at the community center.

Made arrangements for supplies to be brought in and even paid people to house those evacuated. He made sure I got a check to cover my loss. He's a very generous man."

I let out a small sigh, surprised. "Yeah, Mom, He's ... he's not what I expected. I'm so confused."

"Well, honey, sometimes life throws us curveballs. Just remember to trust your instincts. You've always had a good head on your shoulders," she advises, in her reassuring warm voice. "If he's right for you, you'll know."

"That's the problem. I don't usually date guys like him."

"What do you mean?"

"He lives halfway across the country."

"You've dated men that don't live in Leavenworth before."

Finally, I confess, "Mom, the fire has brought up my memories of Derek."

"Honey, you can't let what happened to Derek ruin your chances of finding happiness again. He would want you to find someone else."

I let out a long sigh, emotions swirling inside me. "I know you're right. Derek would want me to be happy. But my heart still feels his loss."

"Of course it does, sweetie. You two had something very special."

Tears spring to my eyes as memories of Derek flood my mind—our first date, moving in together, his surprise proposal. A sob catches in my throat.

"What if I can never have that again, Mom?"

"Oh, honey," Mom says gently. "I know it doesn't feel like it now, but you will love again. Maybe not exactly the same way, but that doesn't mean it can't be just as wonderful."

I dab at my wet cheeks, comforted by her words. Still, the grief feels raw.

Mom continues, "Mark sounds like a good man. Just get to know him, without expectations or comparisons. See where it goes. You deserve to be happy."

I take a deep, steadying breath. "Yeah … you're right, Mom. I should give this thing with Mark a chance, without putting pressure on it to be anything specific." Just saying the words lifts a weight from my shoulders I didn't realize I was carrying.

"There you go. One step at a time, sweetheart," Mom says. "I'm always here if you want to talk more."

"Thanks, Mom." With her support, maybe I can finally leave the door open to new love instead of hiding behind my grief and fear.

We talk a little more, mostly about trivial things. As we say our goodbyes, I feel a little lighter, a little more grounded. Mom's calls always have that effect on me. They remind me of where I come from, of the strength and resilience that's been instilled in me.

I lie back down, the conversation with Mom swirling in my mind alongside everything else. I also make a mental note to call the doctor for a check-up soon. I've been warned about hypoglycemia and its effects. I've been through so much lately. It's definitely time to deal with it.

Chapter Eleven

Mark

As I fly over the open fields, all I can think about is Amber. How she's touched me in so many ways. She is so unlike the women I've dated before. Definitely different from my ex-wife, Veronica, who's been nothing but trouble since the day we met. After that fiasco, I never wanted to get mixed up in another woman's life again. I swore off relationships after the nightmare of my marriage ended. My ex was selfish, entitled, and manipulative— basically sucked me dry emotionally. By the time we split, I was bitter and wary of ever letting another woman get close.

But there's something about Amber that goes straight to my heart, which scares the hell out of me. She somehow manages to chip away at the protective walls I've built around my heart. When I talk to her, I open up about things I usually keep hidden.

Maybe with Amber I can finally leave the ghosts of my past behind for good. The future is still unclear, but one thing I know for sure—that woman has awakened feelings in me I never thought possible. I don't know how this will all play out. I don't know if a man like me can fit into Amber's world or if she'd ever want to be part of mine. For the first time in my life, I'm willing to find out. I'm willing to slow down, breathe, and let this unexpected, uncharted feeling lead me wherever it goes.

My cell phone unexpectedly buzzes with an incoming call. Strange to get service this high up. I put the plane on autopilot and answer it.

"Mark, thank God I reached you!" Melissa practically shouts through the phone.

Before I can say hello, she launches into a rapid-fire account, "Mark you need to get back here asap. Someone is trying to sabotage your upcoming Chicago deal."

"What are you talking about?"

"We've received threats that if we don't withdraw from the deal, some unfavorable information about your past could show up on the news, dragging your reputation through the mud."

As soon as my wheels touch down, I race directly from the airport to my downtown Houston high-rise headquarters. I brush past the front desk attendant and head straight for the elevators, jabbing impatiently at the floor button.

When I finally arrive at my corner executive office, I find Melissa's face creased with worry. Before I can even set my suitcase down, my VP of Operations, Carter, blurts out, "I have information you should know about. My assistant was contacted while you were gone by your ex asking questions about you—your net worth, assets tied up in overseas projects, anything that could impact this business," he reveals.

I'm stunned by the mention of my ex.

Carter continues, "It seems Veronica's recently connected on social media with a muckraking reporter claiming that you were hiding some dealings in the past. The timing is ... unsettling."

"You are kidding me."

"There's more. I had my team do some digging. Veronica still retains financial stakes in Capstone Enterprises—our biggest rival for the Chicago Plaza contract," he explains. "This information may sink our chances if not handled properly."

My pulse races as I pace the office. "Veronica was always one to hold a grudge but sabotaging my company's most important bid—that seems beyond vindictive! We need to stop her!"

I feel myself getting worked up all over again, envisioning Veronica smugly getting the last laugh if she wins this bid by defaming me.

I turn silently to gaze out my floor-to-ceiling windows, downtown Houston gleaming under gloomy skies that match my mood. The view from this corner office usually thrills me, reminding me how far I've climbed. But today, staring at the chrome and glass monuments to my success provides little comfort.

Now with Veronica and the darker chapters of my past conspiring to bring me down, I strain to glimpse the future, but only see threats—my empire, my hopes with Amber, all jeopardized unless I can outmaneuver Veronica once and for all.

Over the next forty-eight hours, I barely sleep, consumed

with strategizing my next move. My team works around the clock, but I still can't shake a sense of paranoia that my budding romance and my company's future might be wrecked if I can't quash this brewing PR storm.

Playing up my help in Leavenworth, we set in motion the public perception issues of a caring company. I know Amber isn't going to be happy about my mentioning the fire near Leavenworth again, but I am sincere about doing what I can for her town.

* * *

I reach for the phone, a mix of anticipation and nervousness swirling within me. It's Amber's voice I want to hear, Amber I need to talk to.

The moment she answers, a wave of relief washes over me. "I miss you," I say, the words slipping out more easily than I expect.

She replies, "I miss you, too," sending a thrill through me.

"When are you coming back?" she asks.

It's a question that's been haunting me now that I'm here. The answer is tied up in responsibilities and commitments I can't escape. "Soon," I reply. "Are you still out there fighting the fire?"

"Yes."

"God, I wish you'd let someone else take care of the fire."

"It means a lot to me."

"You are one stubborn woman."

As we talk, I grapple with the reality of my emotions. Falling for Amber wasn't something I'd planned, but as I hang on to every word she says, I realize it's not something I can—or even want to—fight against.

"Goodnight, Mark."

"Goodnight." After I hang up my thoughts linger on her, on us—the fear of will happen if she learns about my past.

* * *

"They weren't happy you postponed the meeting." Melissa drops the file on my desk.

I stare at the file. With this PR crisis, I almost forgot how much time I'll be spending in Chicago if I win this contract. *Shit.* What am I going to tell Amber?

I need to be fully present to pull this deal off. What have I gotten myself into? I motion for Melissa to leave, and I turn my back to the door.

Picking up the phone, I dial, then put the call on speaker.

"Hey, Buddy. What's up?" Ethan's familiar voice booms.

"How's Hawaii?" I look out the window at the clouds.

"I don't think you called for a weather report."

"I hate to bother you." I drum my fingers on the desk nervously.

"I know you wouldn't call if it wasn't important."

"I've gotten myself into a situation and honestly don't know what direction to go."

"Well, that's a first. I may not be able to help, but run it past me."

"It's about Kim's sister, Amber."

I hear his laughter in the background. "You are calling me about female problems? This is a first. 'Mr. never gets involved with a woman.'"

"I know. It's complicated. You know we went on that hike, and while I was up there ... I don't know if it was just mountains and fresh air, but she got to me."

"Got to you?"

Not knowing how to say it any other way, I just spit it out, "I think I'm falling in love with her."

"Seriously?"

"Yeah, and it's mucking up my life."

"Welcome to the club. How does Amber feel about you?"

"I believe she's got feelings for me, too, but she's not keen on a long-distance relationship. And I can tell there is no way in hell I'll be able to convince her to move in with me out here."

"Humm. Her roots are deep in Leavenworth. She has a business there, too."

"With the fire going on, she's dedicated all her time to the community. I'm worried about her. I don't like knowing she's out there."

"I understand. So, are you in Houston now?"

"Yes, but I've got a project in Chicago I've been working on. It's worth a hell of a lot of money if I pull it off."

"Wow, congratulations."

"But it will mean me staying there for a while, and I'm afraid I'll lose Amber in the process. And to top it off, Veronica tipped off a guy about a project I did in the past that I'm not proud of. If Amber gets wind of it, she'll never speak to me again."

"That's tough. I guess the question is, how much do you care about Amber? Is she just a passing phase, or do you see something more with her?"

"I'm afraid to let myself go there. We live in different worlds. Everything seems so impossible at the moment."

"Well, you need to figure that out. But let me give you a word of advice I learned the hard way. If you love her and walk away, you'll regret it and be miserable for the rest of your life.

Loving someone means sacrificing some of the things you think you need but don't. You need to ask yourself how much money you want in the bank. Mark, you are already one of the richest people in the country. You can't buy love and happiness. You have to grab it when it comes."

"Thanks, Ethan. You made your point. I'll think about it."

"You bet."

I hang up and turn to find my ex-wife standing in the doorway. "Shit," I mutter.

"Well, well. Mark's got a girlfriend. Who would've guessed?"

"I tried to stop her, but she barged in." Melissa stands there, annoyed.

"What are you doing here?" I stare at Veronica, anger rising inside me. She looks far too smug, eavesdropping on my private conversation. "I asked what you're doing here," I repeat through gritted teeth.

"I came by to chat about old times," Veronica says, sauntering farther into my office, her high heels clicking on the floor.

"You and I have nothing to talk about."

"Oh, come on Mark, don't be like that." She perches on the edge of my desk, crossing her long legs slowly. I've seen this act before. She's trying to toy with me.

"I want you to leave. Now." I stand up, glaring down at her. She doesn't flinch.

"Not until you and I have a little talk. You've been a very bad boy lately, spying on me." Her voice takes on a patronizing tone.

I laugh. "Are you seriously trying to scold me? You're unbelievable."

"I warned you not to cross me, Mark," Veronica snaps,

dropping her flirtatious act. "You should know by now I always get my way."

"Not this time." I grab her arm and yank her off my desk. She stumbles slightly in her too-high heels but catches herself.

"Don't you dare touch me," she hisses.

"Then get the hell out and don't come back," I snarl. How did I not see this vindictive side of her before we got married? Or maybe she's gotten worse since the divorce.

Veronica straightens herself, smoothing down her clothes and hair. The smug look is back.

"You haven't heard the last from me," she says coolly. "That little girlfriend of yours won't want anything to do with you when she finds out what a heartless bastard you are."

With that, she turns on her heels and stalks out. I resist the urge to go after her. Then I sink down into my chair, head spinning. I have to warn Amber about Veronica before she gets to her. But I can't focus on that now.

I take a few deep breaths to calm myself. That woman still knows how to get under my skin, even after all these years. I can't let her distract me right now, though.

I pick up my phone and dial Amber's number. It goes straight to voicemail. I debate leaving a message warning her about Veronica, but I don't want to worry her if I don't have to. Hopefully, Veronica's just bluffing about contacting her.

"Hey, Amber, it's Mark," I say after the beep. "Give me a call when you get a chance. I may have to stay in Chicago for work, but I want to talk to you before I finalize anything. Hope you're staying safe with the fires and all. Okay, talk to you soon."

I hang up, feeling anxious about being apart from Amber for weeks or months, with Veronica plotting against me. But the Chicago Plaza Hotel deal is too lucrative to pass up. I can't throw it all away now.

Just then, my assistant Melissa pops her head in. "They're here."

I nod, taking another deep breath. I have to compartmentalize for now—focus on work so I can nail this deal. Then I can figure out what the hell to do about Veronica and Amber.

"Send them in." I straighten my tie and put my business face on, pushing all emotional turmoil aside. This is what I've trained myself to do for years. I just pray this deal doesn't ruin everything in the process.

Here goes nothing.

I stride into the conference room with my usual air of confidence, shaking hands with the investors. I pour on the charm as we make small talk before getting down to business. My mind keeps wandering back to Amber, though.

I wonder if she's gotten my message yet. Is she out battling fires, putting her own safety at risk to help others? Guilt eats at me for not being there with her.

"Shall we discuss the specifics of the development?" one of the investors says, pulling my attention back to the meeting.

I nod, opening my laptop to bring up the 3D renderings of the luxury high-rise we want to build and project the images on the screen for them to see. As I launch into my presentation, a notification pops up at the bottom of my screen.

My heart leaps when I see it's an incoming call from Amber. This deal needs to come first right now. Still, seeing her name fuels my determination to wrap this up quickly so I can call her back.

"As you'll see from the plans, we intend to have 200 high-end rooms, multiple restaurants with 5-star chefs ..." I continue detailing all the lavish features that I know will appeal to the luxury hospitality market in Chicago.

The investors pepper me with questions, which I handle smoothly, anticipating their concerns. After an intense back and forth, I can see I have them on the hook. We just need to reel them in carefully now.

My phone lights up with another call from Amber. It's taking all my willpower not to excuse myself from this meeting. Just a little longer, I tell myself, then I can call her back.

I wrap up the meeting an hour later. They appear interested but have another offer to consider. I'll just have to wait for their answer.

As soon as they leave, I scramble for my cell phone. Two more missed calls from Amber. My heart is pounding. The weight of my feelings for Amber presses heavily against my chest, a mixture of anticipation and a peculiar nervousness. With a deep breath, I press the call button, pretending to myself more than anyone that this is just another regular call.

The phone rings, and for a brief moment, I imagine her face lighting up as she sees my name flashing on her screen. It's a comforting thought, one that brings a smile to my lips.

She answers on the first ring.

"Hey, Amber," I start, trying to keep my voice even, to mask the depth of emotion swirling within me. The simple act of hearing her voice, soft and familiar, sends an unexpected jolt of warmth through me.

"Hey! I'm so glad you called," Amber says, sounding relieved but out of breath. "Sorry I missed your earlier call. Things have been non-stop crazy here."

"Don't worry about it," I reply. "I'm just glad you're okay. Are you in the middle of fighting fires right now?"

"Yeah, we just contained part of it, but there are still active hotspots flaring up in different places. I only have a quick break to return calls. Did you say you have to stay there? Does that mean you won't be flying back here anytime soon?"

I hesitate, guilt flooding through me for not being there for her.

"There's a work opportunity I've bid on," I say carefully. "But I wanted to talk to you before finalizing it. With everything going on there, I don't feel right being halfway across the country from you."

"Well, that's your life, Mark. This is why it will never work between us."

"Please don't say that."

"What do you want me to say? It's not like we are in a committed relationship."

She's right, but I don't want to lose her. "I'm nuts about you. I would do anything ..."

She cuts me off. "That's not true. If you really care about me, you'd be here to hug me after my day on the fire lines instead of in your cushy office making deals that will require you to never have time to see me."

"I'm sorry."

"So am I." Amber sniffs, and I can tell she's crying. "Goodbye, Mark."

The line goes dead. I drop my head into my hands. Then I get up and fling the file on this Chicago Hotel deal across the room. Ethan is right. If I cared enough for Amber, I'd be willing to make sacrifices to make the relationship work. He gave up his career for Kim. Would I be able to give up this deal for Amber?

Chapter Twelve

Mark

I knock on the heavy oak door of Veronica's ultra-modern high-rise apartment. Soft dance music plays from within. My stomach churns with unease as I wait on her doorstep. Meeting here instead of at a restaurant or coffee shop is a bad idea. But I need discretion to make this deal.

The door swings open, and I catch my breath. Veronica stands framed in the doorway, dressed in a low-cut, silk, black dress with a split up the side. I swallow hard. Her auburn hair cascades over her shoulders, and a coy smile plays on her bright red lips. She's intentionally trying to throw me off balance and awaken old desires. I shift my eyes away from her.

"I was surprised when you called, Mark. Please come in," she purrs. "Is there something I can do for you?"

I brush past her into the dimly lit living room, the modern artwork and angular furniture cold and impersonal like

Veronica herself. The heavy door clicks shut behind me. I turn to face her, inhaling her familiar floral perfume now mingled with the aroma of flickering scented candles around the room. The space is dark and seductive.

"Wine?" she asks in a silken voice, sauntering over to her well-stocked bar.

"Scotch." I need something strong if I'm going to make it through this negotiation.

She arches an eyebrow. "Oh, I like that you want the hard stuff tonight." Her stilettos click on the floor as she pours me two fingers of amber liquid over ice into a cut-crystal glass. I take it from her outstretched hand, her sharp red nails grazing my skin.

I let out a breath and make my way to the leather couch.

"How's what's her name?" Veronica asks, her voice dripping with disdain as she sinks onto the couch beside me. She crosses her long legs, and the slit reveals pale smooth skin almost to her hip. She's playing games. Trying to seduce me, as she did countless times during our turbulent marriage.

I clench my jaw and don't answer, staring into the amber liquor as I swirl the ice cubes around.

"Charming, I'm sure. And naïve, I bet." She takes a slow sip of her wine, eyeing me over the rim of her glass. "Does she know how heartless you can be?"

"Shut up," I snap, the scotch burning in my throat as I take a gulp.

"How about your past?" She sets down her glass with a knowing smile.

I don't answer.

"Does she know about us? That I can still make you tremble with just a whisper of my name?" Veronica adjusts her body closer to mine. "Or is that your little secret, too?"

My heart races as memories flood back to Veronica's dangerous dance of passion and betrayal. My mouth is dry from nerves. I take another sip, the ice clinking against the crystal.

"She doesn't need to know anything," I finally say, my voice laced with defiance.

Veronica laughs, sending shivers down my spine. "Oh, darling, secrets have a way of coming to light. And when they do, I wonder ... Will she still want you?"

I lean forward on the cushion. "Veronica, how about you keep your distance from Amber, and I'll make you a deal?"

Her eyes flash with curiosity. "Ooh, what kind of deal?" She runs her tongue over her upper lip.

I take a deep breath. "I'll let you have the Chicago Plaza Hotel contract if you promise to never contact Amber."

"You must be serious about her if you're willing to do that." She arches an eyebrow, toying with the diamond pendant resting in the hollow of her throat.

I just stare at her with my jaw clenched. This contract would be my most prestigious one yet—and I'm handing it over to my manipulative ex-wife. I must be out of my mind.

"Is that all you can offer?" she asks with a coy tilt of her head. "Anything else you can sweeten the deal with?"

"Like what?"

She sets down her wine glass with a sharp clink and slides closer, her silk dress exposing more than I wish to see. She brings her lips close to my ear, her breath hot and sweet. "Oh, I don't know. How about you spend the night ... for old time's sake?"

I shudder as she starts unbuttoning my shirt. "No!" I grab her wrists, my pulse hammering. "Do you want the damn contract or not?"

Veronica wrenches her wrists from my grasp with a defiant glare. "What? You afraid you might lose control?" She laughs. "I know how much you liked to be in charge."

I don't reply.

"And how do you know I can't win the Chicago development contract without your help?"

I sink back against the cushions, rubbing my temple, my anger building. This woman is infuriating. "Hey, I'm handing it to you on a silver platter here."

"Hmm ..." She taps her chin, eyes gleaming. "This is so unlike you, Mark. Always looking out for number one. How can I be sure you'll keep your word?"

My patience is wearing dangerously thin. I slam my glass down on the coffee table, the ice cubes clinking. "Well, if you want to walk away from a massive commission payday, that's your choice."

I push up from the couch and stride toward the door, eager to escape. Coming here was a mistake. I'll need to find another way to keep Veronica from contacting Amber.

"Wait!" Veronica cries out. I pause with my hand on the door handle. I hear the sharp click of Veronica's heels on the floor behind me. "Okay, you have a deal. I get the Chicago project, and I won't contact your little sweetheart."

I turn to face her. She looks up at me, one hand on her cocked hip, victory shining in her eyes.

"Shake on it?" I extend my hand in offering, wanting this bargain done.

A sly smile spreads across Veronica's face. "Oh, no, baby, I want more than that." She presses closer, trailing a nail down my chest. "I want a kiss. A real kiss to seal the deal."

I've played right into her hands. The bitter taste of that realization is almost too much to bear. She knows it too, the slight upturn of her lips, that glimmer of triumph in her eyes—it's all there, clear as day. I'm aware of her power and how she's always been able to twist my actions to her benefit.

My heart pounds with anger and adrenaline. If it finally gets her out of my life, fine. It's a small price to pay.

I grab her waist roughly and crush my mouth against hers possessively. Our kiss grows more frenzied as we try to dominate one another until it becomes a battlefield of wills, our bodies pressed together like two halves of a shattered, jagged mirror. I can feel her heart racing against my own chest, her breath coming in short, ragged gasps.

Her hands climb under my shirt, and her nails dig into my skin. The sharp pain takes me back to all the moments we've shared. Even though they feel like distant memories now, they are still ingrained within me.

Veronica tugs at my belt.

I pull away, looking into Veronica's eyes. They're pale blue, shallow, and untrustworthy. I can tell she's not just after a bargain—she wants to own me, to drag me back into her web, and I won't let her.

I hold her at arm's length, my hands firmly on her shoulders. Her eyes blaze with a mix of lust and rage. "Don't stop now. I know you want me," she whispers, gasping for breath.

"You've always thought that you owned me, Veronica. But you were wrong then, and you're wrong now."

Veronica's expression hardens, and I know she wants to say something.

I stare at her. "You got your damn kiss."

She grins, pleased with herself.

"Now, you stay the hell out of my life," I demand as I release her.

Her chest heaves, lipstick smeared, as she struggles to regain composure.

I smooth my rumpled shirt, tucking it back in my pants, and run a hand through my hair. I pause to look at her. "The downtown Chicago development contract is as good as yours. I'll contact the investors first thing in the morning."

Veronica is silent, one hand pressed to her swollen lips. Our eyes lock for a tense moment. Her mouth curves into a knowing smile. "You always walk away when things get too hot, don't you, Mark?"

I don't respond. With my heart pounding in my ears, I slip out the door and pull it firmly shut behind me. The cool night air hits my flaming cheeks as I emerge from the building onto the street. For all our toxic history, you'd think I'd know better than to kiss that woman. But that tango ends tonight. Hopefully, I'm rid of her for good.

I have what I need—her promise to leave Amber alone. I take out my phone to arrange a flight back to Washington as soon as possible. Thoughts of Amber's smile and her laughter fill my mind. Let my staff deal with my other clients until I return. I need to clear my head and tell Amber how I feel about her. As I hail a taxi, thoughts of Veronica fade into the past where they belong.

Chapter Thirteen

Amber

I pour myself a cup of coffee and bite into my toast when I hear a pounding on my door. Tightening the tie on my robe, I go to answer it.

"Why are you here? Shouldn't you be off overseas somewhere?"

Mark looks down at me, his eyes searching mine. "Amber, listen to me," he says slowly. "I withdrew from the downtown Chicago Plaza Hotel deal. I'm not here for any reason other than you. I ... I can't live without you in my life. I think I'm falling in love with you."

His confession hangs in the air between us, sending a ripple of shock through me. In love with me? "I don't understand," I stammer, my heart racing. "Why me? You have your life, your business ... I'm not even a city woman."

He lets out a small chuckle, not mocking, but rather one of

disbelief. "Why you? Amber, you're the most incredible woman I've ever met. You're honest, passionate, and brave. How could I not love you?"

I'm at a loss for words. His gaze is intense and sincere. It's hard to reconcile this version of Mark with the one I had in my mind before, the one comfortably dealing with the press, removed from the gritty reality of the fire.

"Mark, I'm ... I'm just a small-town girl. I'm not someone who fits into your world," I say, the words sounding hollow even to my ears.

"That's where you're mistaken," he insists gently. "It's not about fitting into a world. It's about figuring out how we can make this work. And I know this is sudden, but I can't ignore how I feel about you, Amber. I had to tell you."

His words wash over me, sending with them a tide of emotions that I'm afraid to navigate. It's overwhelming.

"Mark, I can't ..." I start, but the words trail off. How do I articulate the jumble of thoughts and feelings inside me? The surprise, the disbelief, the faint flicker of something that might be hope.

"I'm not asking for a commitment now," he says, picking up on my hesitation. "Just ... don't shut me out. Give me a chance to show you how I feel, to be a part of your life."

I look up at him, his face so close to mine, and I allow myself to consider the possibility. What would it mean to let Mark in, to explore these feelings that seem to have sprung up since our hike together?

"I know we've both got stuff to work through. I sure as hell do. But I'm asking you to give us a chance. Will you do that?"

I nod my head.

He starts to lean in, hesitating as if asking permission. Unable to wait, I close the distance, kissing him eagerly. After having pushed him away, having Mark here with me now feels like coming up for air.

He returns the kiss with equal fervor, arms encircling me and pulling me against his chest. We sink back into the couch cushions, lost in each other. All the tension and uncertainty between us seems to melt away.

When we finally break for air, faces flushed and breathing uneven, Mark rests his forehead against mine. "God, I've wanted to do that since I got here," he murmurs.

He plants a row of kisses along my jawline to my ear. "I didn't want to rush you into this." His breath tickles my neck. "But holding back was agony."

I trace my fingers down his back, feeling the heat of his skin through his shirt. "I thought I didn't want this, but having you here ..."

Mark silences me with another searing kiss that steals my breath. We kiss with abandon, hands roaming greedily over each other. I straddle his lap, needing to be as close as possible, to feel every inch of him against me.

His hands slide under my robe, caressing my bare thighs and hips. I ache for more of his touch, for the hardness I can feel growing beneath me.

"Are you feeling up to this? I can stop if you'd rather wait. Do you need to eat something?"

I silence him with a deep kiss, then lean back to meet his dark, desire-filled eyes. "I don't want to eat anything right now. I just want you."

Before he can reply, I climb off his lap and take his hand, leading him toward my bedroom. He follows without resistance.

Once inside, I let my robe slip to the floor, then press

myself against him, reveling in the feel of his clothing against my naked skin.

Mark's mouth finds the sensitive spot on my neck as his hands grip my backside, pulling me tighter to him. "God, you are so beautiful," he whispers hoarsely.

I tug at his shirt. He obliges, stripping off his shirt and jeans with impressive speed. The sight of his muscular physique makes me ache with need. I run my hands over his sculpted arms, chest, and abs, kissing every inch I can reach. I notice scratches on his back. "What happened?"

"What?"

"You have scratches on your back?"

"I do? I must have gotten too close to a tree branch. Yes, I remember getting whacked now when I was getting out of the car the other day."

Mark lifts me effortlessly and lays me on the bed, his warm body covering mine. Our kisses and caresses become more urgent, and our breathing ragged. He does things to me that make me crazy with desire, and I moan.

We move slowly at first, savoring the feeling of finally coming together. But soon, passion overtakes us, and we are lost in a blaze of heat and sensation that consumes everything else.

At last, he enters me slowly, eyes locked on mine. I gasp at the sensation of him filling me so completely.

Afterward, we lie tangled in each other's arms, skin slick with sweat, hearts gradually returning to normal rhythm. Mark trails lazy kisses over my shoulders, and I sigh contentedly. "God, I love you so much," he tells me.

Right now, nothing else matters but being here with him. For this one perfect moment, the chaos and the fire fade away. There's only the two of us.

Chapter Fourteen

Amber

I wince as I climb up the steps of my cabin. Soot and sweat cling to my skin even after shedding my grimy suit at the station. I fumble at the door, aching for a hot shower. But I freeze with my hand on the doorknob. A sleek Mercedes is parked around the side of my house. Who's here? That's not Mark's rental car. I should've locked my cabin door.

I push inside to find an impeccably dressed woman with auburn hair perched on my sofa. She scans my rustic interior with a judgmental glint in her eyes before settling her gaze on me.

"You must be Amber," she says coolly, not bothering to stand. "I'm Veronica. Mark's ex-wife."

My breath catches. "What are you doing here?"

Veronica's lips curve into a smile. She pats the sofa cushion.

"Come sit. I want to tell you something you should know about Mark."

Warily, I sink onto the edge of an armchair, gripping the smooth wooden arms for support.

"Despite being divorced, he still comes to me. When we're together, we can't resist each other. It's as though we are cut from the same cloth. He knows I'm the only person who understands him. When he's struggling, I offer him relief. And this Chicago deal has been a thorn in his side."

I can barely breathe. The air in the room feels too thick, too heavy. Time is slowing, each second stretching out endlessly as she continues.

"Poor Mark." She smiles. "He's weak and needed to let go of his stress, so he offered me the Chicago deal," she says, sounding sympathetic. Then she lowers her voice and reaches out to me. "I thought you deserved to know that night before he flew back here, Mark came to me, and we made love."

The words hang between us as I struggle to comprehend this version of Mark that Veronica paints.

"How could he?" I whisper, more to myself than to her.

The front door suddenly bangs open. Mark charges in, his gaze darts between us.

"Damn it, Veronica!" He runs a hand through his dark hair. "We had an agreement. You were never to contact Amber. What the hell are you doing here?"

"Hi, Darling. That deal you offered fell through, so I thought I would visit your girlfriend and let her know how we consummated your departure."

His eyes flash with anger. He turns to me, his expression pleading. But to Veronica, he shouts, "That's a lie, and you know it!"

I shy away, stunned and overwhelmed. I don't know what to believe.

"Oh, I beg to disagree." Veronica reclines back with a satisfied smile. "Show her the scratches I made on your back."

I close my eyes, drawing a shaky breath. He told me they were from a tree branch.

I stand with my fists clenched at my sides. "I think you should both leave."

Mark's eyes widen. "Amber, please ..." He reaches for me, but I step back, the wounded look on his face cutting me deeply. "I gave her my Chicago deal so I could be with you."

I wrap my arms around myself with my gaze lowered. I care for him deeply. And he seems sincere. But doubt still gnaws at me. Is this awful woman telling the truth? Where did he get those scratches? Did he sleep with her before coming to me?

"I think you've shown your true colors, Mark," Veronica interjects coolly. She stands and smooths the wrinkles from her skirt. "You should give Amber space to process things. Come along now."

She brushes past him toward the door. Mark hesitates, his eyes searching my face.

"Go," I whisper.

Veronica's car engine rumbles to life outside my window and fades into the distance.

Mark steps toward me. "Amber, please believe me. Veronica is lying. She wants to destroy what we have. I didn't have sex with her. I swear to God."

I hold up a hand, silencing him. My head throbs and I'm close to tears. I cannot handle explanations and excuses right now.

"Just go," I repeat quietly. I turn my back with my arms crossed protectively over my chest.

For a moment, the only sounds are the aged floorboards creaking as Mark hesitates. I stare at the exposed timber beams crisscrossing the vaulted ceiling overhead and breathe through the painful squeeze around my heart.

Finally, I hear footsteps, then the click of the front door closing. I lower myself onto the sofa, Veronica's floral perfume still in the air, and burst into tears.

Chapter Fifteen

Mark

The phone rings once, twice, ten times before Amber's bubbly voicemail message picks up. I hang up without leaving a word, just as I have the last four attempts.

I rake a hand through my hair and resume pacing my hotel room. I look out my window. Below, a few people wander the streets of Leavenworth. The air is thick with an ashen haze covering the tables and flowers along the street. Most of the tourists have left for places with cleaner air to breathe.

Why won't she answer? I need to talk to her. Try to explain things after the ambush from hell, courtesy of my deranged ex-wife.

The moment I saw Amber shrinking from me at her cabin, it felt like the ground dropped open beneath my feet. In that split second, I clearly realized how much I stand to lose if she writes me off because of Veronica's thirst for vengeance.

This can't be happening. Not when I just worked up the nerve to acknowledge how deeply I care about her. Loving someone this much feels foreign and terrifying. But also exhilarating in ways I've never experienced before. Amber makes me want to be a better man. I can't stomach losing that now. Not when I'm finally glimpsing the man I could become after my time volunteering at the community center.

The phone stays silent despite my relentless calls. As the day fades into a stark, lonely evening, I make up my mind. Throwing on my jacket, I head out into the night. I'm going over there to plead my case, even if she tries to shut me out. She at least owes me a chance to come clean about everything.

A half-hour later, I pull up beside Amber's car on the secluded mountain road. Her cabin windows emit a warm glow against the dark tree line.

Before I lose my nerve, I stride up the walkway and knock on the weathered timber door. Footsteps approach from within. My breath stalls in my chest. Please, just give me a chance to explain, I pray.

The door swings open—but instead of Amber, an older woman with a halo of silver hair and familiar warm eyes blinks at me in surprise.

"Mark, how nice to see you! I'm Martha, Amber's mother. We met at Kim's wedding, remember?"

I clear my throat, willing my voice not to shake. "Sorry for just dropping by, but it's important I speak to Amber. Is she here? We had a ... misunderstanding earlier."

Martha smiles, stepping out onto the small, covered porch with me and closing the door behind her. My heart drops. Clearly, I'm not allowed inside.

"Yes, Amber told me there was an incident with your ex-wife," Martha replies. She must read the desperation on my face because she touches my arm. "Just give her a little time, Mark. I know my daughter, and I can tell she cares deeply for you, too."

I nod. I've spent my whole life avoiding vulnerability, hiding behind arrogant charm and wealth as shields. But here, stripped bare under the stars with her mother's compassionate eyes on me, I'm closer to the boy I was before life's losses hardened me— desperately wishing on every dandelion puff for the faintest chance of something good in this world. While in the air around me, the sound of gunshots cracked, and people fell in the streets covered in blood.

Martha gestures to a wooden bench nestled among the pine trees nearby. "Why don't you come sit with me? I'll make us some tea."

Soon, we're seated side by side, steam rising from the mugs cupped in our palms. The night air has a biting edge, but Martha's maternal warmth cuts through the cold. I've craved this without even knowing it—the simplicity of human kindness. I know now why Amber is so uniquely extraordinary. She comes from a loving family.

I take a slow sip, gathering my words. "Did Amber tell you why Veronica, my ex-wife, came here earlier?"

Martha shakes her head, wispy curls fluttering in the breeze. "Only that it had to do with your relationship history. But honestly ..." She meets my eyes directly. "The details don't matter to me. The way Amber talks about you ... I haven't seen her eyes shine for anyone like that since Derek died."

I cling to that spark of hope, my voice strained. "You think she will listen to me?"

"She will. Just be patient, and when she's ready, tell her what you need to. Amber can handle the truth."

The knots in my chest loosen. My next breath comes a little easier.

Chapter Sixteen

Mark

As I pick up the phone, Veronica's voice oozes through the speaker, "Hello, sweetheart," in that cloying tone of hers.

"I thought we had a deal that you were never to contact Amber," I snap back, unable to contain my anger. "I withdrew my bid on the Chicago project so you could have it. And you show up spouting lies to Amber. You are a devious piece of shit, you know that?"

"Well, it seems they preferred dealing directly with you and got wind that I was behind your pulling out. Did someone from your office leak that to destroy my chances?"

I pause, taking a moment to cool my simmering rage. "Or maybe they thought you weren't up to the task. Ever think of that?"

She laughs. "Oh, come on, Mark. We both know how this game is played."

Without another word, I end the call. I'm done with the games, the lies, and letting my past with Veronica haunt me. It's gone on too long, and I'm finished letting her dangle stuff over my head.

I pace back and forth across the room. My mind races, thoughts tangling and untangling. I grab my phone again, this time dialing my assistant.

As soon as Melissa answers, I get straight to the point. "Call a press conference at our Chicago office."

There's a pause on the other end. "Why?"

I stop pacing. "I want to let the world know about the Wilshire Heights deal," I say.

There's a moment of silence as she processes my unexpected request. "Are you sure about this?"

"Definitely."

"Okay. If that's what you want."

"Yep." I grab my keys and head for the door to fly back to Texas to get ready for my Chicago ordeal.

I think back to when I first bought the Wilshire Heights property. I was young, ambitious, and hungry for success. Tearing down the low-rent apartments and replacing them with a fancy high-rise seemed like an easy way to make a quick profit. Still, I didn't fully consider the consequences of my actions. I grew up in a place just like the one I was demolishing and knew what life was like living there—people on welfare, always short on money and food. I remember the day the tenants were forced to leave, their faces filled with anger and despair. I pushed the memory away. Unfortunately, it always lingered in the back of my mind. But I didn't want to appear soft and weak to my peers back then. As time went on, I just learned not to think about anything but the money I was making.

Amber's awakened me to the fact I've been running my whole life, avoiding my true feelings, never wanting to be vulnerable. Seeing those people at the community center reminded me of the hardships other people endure. They aren't just numbers on a spreadsheet but breathing human beings with feelings and families. And Amber's putting herself in danger to protect the lives and homes of her community. What have I ever contributed to society?

Here I am, tearing down places considered worthless, replacing them with expensive buildings catering to the rich.

I stand up and walk to the window, looking out at the city skyline. From those early, hungry days to now, it's been a journey. I wonder how many people suffered because of developers like me.

A knock at the door pulls me from my thoughts. It's my assistant. I signal for her to enter.

"Everything's ready for tomorrow morning, Mark," she informs me, handing over a folder.

I thank her and flip through the pages, my eyes scanning the information. "Good. I want to make sure we have a clear message. I'm not trying to make excuses for what I did. However, I want people to understand that I'm committed to doing better in the future."

My thoughts are already darting to the many ways this could unfold.

* * *

With a deep breath, I brace myself for what's coming. The buzz of anticipation hangs heavy in the air as I step up to the podium, the glare of the camera lights stark against the backdrop of the conference room of our Chicago office. I clear my throat, steadying my nerves. This is it—the moment to face the music, to confront the consequences of the Wilshire Heights deal head-on.

"Good morning," I begin, my voice steady despite the turmoil inside me. "I've called you here today to address the past decisions made regarding the Wilshire Heights property, and more importantly, the impact of those decisions on the lives of its residents."

"That was ten years ago. Why now?" a voice asks.

"Because tearing down low-income housing is not something I want my company to be known for."

A hand shoots up from the crowd, a reporter from a major TV news channel. "Mr. Harrison, do you believe that your actions regarding Wilshire Heights were justified, considering the displacement of numerous families?"

The question hits hard, but I'm prepared. "Justified? No. At the time, I was driven by ambition and a narrow view of success. It's clear to me now how those actions impacted families and the community in a negative way. And for that, I am deeply sorry."

Another reporter, this one from a local TV station, jumps in. "What specific steps are you taking to rectify the situation? Apologies are one thing, but actions speak louder."

I nod, acknowledging the weight of the question. "You're absolutely right. An apology is just the start. We're launching a community redevelopment fund aimed at supporting not only those displaced by the Wilshire Heights project but other projects as well. This includes affordable housing initiatives and financial assistance to help those affected to find new homes. It's about making right what we got wrong and contributing to the community's wellbeing."

A buzz of murmurs ripples through the room as journalists scribble notes and adjust their cameras. The next question comes from an online news outlet known for its critical take on redevelopment projects. "Mr. Harrison, how can the public trust that your future projects won't repeat the mistakes of Wilshire Heights?"

"It's a fair question," I admit, locking eyes with the questioner. "Transparency and community engagement will be at the heart of everything we do moving forward. We're committing to public consultations and involving community leaders in our planning processes. It's about building trust through consistent, positive action and ensuring our projects benefit everyone, not just the bottom line."

As the press conference continues, questions keep coming. But with every answer, I feel a sense of weight lifting.

Chapter Seventeen

Mark

I'm pretty sure Amber didn't see my press conference on the news, or I would've heard from her. She's not one to watch TV or check the news sites on her phone, either. So, she's not aware of what I just announced.

I'm tired of waiting. I try calling Amber, but her phone goes straight to voicemail again. Inside, I'm just like that frightened kid at the community center who was waiting to find out if his house was lost in the flames.

She's probably out on the fire line today. I head to the station to see if she's there.

When I arrive, I spot a van being loaded up, ready to head out. I go inside the station and find a couple of firefighters suiting up.

"Do you know where Amber Holloway is working today?"

"Yeah, the same place we are headed to."

"I'm Mark Harrison. Can I catch a ride? It's important that I talk to her," I tell them.

One smiles. "Are you the guy who's been handing out money to the town?"

Embarrassed, I smile. "Yeah."

The other guy snickers then says, "Sorry, buddy. You'll have to talk to her when her shift is done. We don't want untrained people getting in the way. It's not safe, and it's against the rules."

"Sure."

I watch them go back to their conversation, ignoring me. I'm about to leave when I notice a uniform hanging on a hook nearby—a fire-resistant coat and pants. When their backs are turned, I grab the gear and slip it on over my clothes, copping a helmet.

Outside, other firefighters are milling around the van, waiting for the ride to the fire line. I casually stroll over and join them. When the driver comes out, we all clamber aboard. I smile, determined to find Amber. She'll probably be furious. But I need to see her face-to-face.

The smoke hits my nostrils first—an acrid, choking smell that invades the van as we bounce along the ragged access road. I peer out the dirty window beside me, my eyes watering. In the distance beyond the trees, a dull orange glow permeates the late afternoon haze. We must be getting close.

My exhilaration at successfully sneaking along on this ride is fading, replaced by nerves and uncertainty. I don't even know what I'll say when I find Amber out here. But ever since her mother hinted Amber might be willing to hear me out if I lay all my cards on the table, I haven't been able to stand the waiting game a minute longer.

We round a bend, and the fire comes into full view through

the trees about a quarter mile off. It reminds me of news footage—chaotic, spreading, alive. The very air around us seems to vibrate with energy. We're close enough now to hear the periodic crack and groan of falling burning timber. Columns of smoke obscure the fading sunlight filtering through the canopy high above.

I glance around at the other passengers jostling shoulders in the cramped truck bed—men and women with faces framed by their protective gear. This is Amber's world now whenever she's out here. My sleek corner office existence feels mundane by comparison.

The truck jolts and slows, pulling off the narrow road to join a handful of other vehicles clustered in a makeshift staging area. Dust swirls as everyone climbs out, and I follow. We're only a few hundred yards from a wall of flames now. The blast of heat is immediate.

People move with purpose amidst the controlled chaos. I catch sight of a row of fire engines parked to one side, firefighters shouting to each other over the roar as they work a pumping hose from one truck's tank. A large water tanker approaches us, rumbling heavily over the uneven ground.

Unsure what to do, I meander slowly behind the others from my truck toward the fire line. The radio chatters updates along with surrounding voices shouting orders. The fire is chewing steadily through bone-dry underbrush. If it's not contained soon, scores of homes that lie directly in its path down the mountain will burn.

I pass the busy pumper trucks and approach a makeshift incident trailer. White fog hangs low, evidence of aerial water drops that did little to slow the flames. The fire is still moving, hungry.

Squinting against the swirling winds and smoke, I search

every passing face for Amber but don't see her. Doubt creeps in. What will I even say if I find her out here? That I'm sorry for keeping secrets? That nearly losing her made me realize how desperately in love with her I am? She'll surely resent me for distracting her from her vital duties. Maybe coming here is a mistake.

Just then, a voice shouts my name over the chaotic noise. I turn to see Amber's friend, Ken Ryder, walking toward me, wearing the same protective gear.

"What the hell are you doing here?" he demands. Before I can respond, he points off to my right, where a distant chain of firefighters is moving steadily away, holding a hose, aiming water at the flames. "You see that crew over there? Go make yourself useful—help them pull that line."

With that, he pivots and marches off, already yelling at someone else. No time or attention to waste on an outsider. Message received. I'm not wanted here unless I'm willing to join the fight.

Squaring my shoulders, I set off toward the distant crew. The roar intensifies the closer I get to the front lines. Concentrated jets of water cut through the smoke like laser beams ahead, hissing and steaming when they hit the tower of flames.

I grab a section of the hose, making myself part of the team. Without a word, they adjust to make space for me in the line. Up close now, I can feel the intense waves of heat. It's like walking slowly toward the open mouth of a furnace. I grit my teeth and focus on keeping the heavy hose elevated at waist height with the others.

Marching steadily forward with our watery ammunition trained on the flames, we hold our tenuous position this way, containing a small section. Progress inches at a time. Sweat soaks through my shirt inside my gear. I ignore the discomfort, consumed with scanning the area for Amber whenever I get the chance.

Eventually, I hear a familiar voice behind me—strong, confident, and unmistakable. "Hey, Mark! With me, let's go!"

I glance back to see Amber waving me out of the line. Hands quickly shuffle to cover my absence, and I scramble toward her, pulse racing. Her face is half obscured by her helmet and dust mask, but her beautiful eyes flash as she grasps my arm firmly. She leads me away from the front down a ragged deer trail into the forest. Soon, the sounds of crackling fire fade, leaving only distant radio chatter and the crunch of underbrush beneath our boots. We pass crews taking a water break in the hazy dusk light filtering through the needled canopy high overhead. The air cools a few degrees.

When we're well away from the staging area, Amber finally stops and turns to face me, hands propped on her hips. "One of the guys told me you snuck aboard the van. Damn it, Mark. Do you have any idea how dangerous this is for an untrained person?" Despite her sharp words, concern lines her expression.

I open my mouth, but she cuts me off. "Please don't make me worry about your safety right now on top of everything else going on out here. I can barely think straight as it is!" Her voice cracks with emotion. Seeing Amber's strong exterior falter stirs a painful squeeze in my chest. I reach tentatively for her hand. After a moment, she allows me to take it.

"You're right, I'm sorry," I say earnestly. "I wasn't thinking. But I had to see you. You haven't returned my calls. And I wanted to talk to you so you'd understand ..."

I trail off at the shine of tears in her eyes as she searches my face.

I continue quietly. "These past few days of nearly losing

you, it's made me see—I don't want to hide parts of myself anymore. Not from you. You deserve the whole truth about my past, and especially Veronica. You deserve the chance to decide if …" I have to pause and steady my own shaky voice. "If I'm someone, you could take another shot on. Because you mean everything to me, Amber."

Amber looks silently back at me for a long moment. In the distance, wood cracks and pops. Radio static filters through the trees.

Finally, Amber nods slowly, blinking her wet eyes. "Okay. I think I'd like to hear the full story." Her face clouds again. "But we'll have plenty of time later. I need to get back on the line."

I squeeze her hand before letting her go. "I know. And I'm sorry for distracting you from such important work." I offer a tentative, hopeful smile. "I just needed you to know I'm here, ready to talk whenever you want. No more holding back. I promise."

Amber takes a long look at me, her shoulders relaxing just slightly. The hint of a smile on her lips. "We'll talk soon," she agrees. With a swift kiss to my cheek, she turns and starts making her way back toward the blaze. I watch until she disappears into the smoke rising through the dark trunks surrounding me. The woods seem to sigh, a light breeze rustling.

Chapter Eighteen

Amber

After seeing Mark here, I can't shake the feeling that something's shifted. And I'm not sure yet what that means for me or what comes next. I am saddened by the loss of so much —Derek, the trees, neighbors' homes. But I can rise above this. That's who I am—a fighter, a survivor.

The heat is oppressive as I swing my axe, clearing away brush near the fire's edge. We have to widen this barrier to stop the flames from spreading farther into the surrounding forest. The smoke stings my eyes as I hack away.

"Help," I hear a voice call out on my radio. It's Shane, one of my fellow firefighters.

Hotspots have sprung up in random areas, bringing new threats to the surrounding woods. I know others have heard Shane's cry for help, too, but I'm closest. I delve into an area I shouldn't go alone. Thick plumes of smoke blot out the sun, raining hot embers down on me as I race desperately through the burning forest. I have to reach Shane before it's too late. His panicked call over the radio echoes hauntingly in my mind, and I have flashes of Derek in our burning house. Shane is one of our own, and I will never abandon him. I radio a distress call with my location, then plunge ahead into the smoke, calling his name.

Suddenly, I spot Shane lying beneath a massive tree trunk, where partially charred branches are pinning his legs at an odd angle. I rush over, immediately assessing the situation. Shane is unresponsive—likely from inhaling too much smoke.

I grasp the thick tree trunk and heave with all my strength. It barely budges. The intense heat is making me lightheaded, but I can't give up. Leveraging my back and legs, I try again, adrenaline fueling my efforts.

Slowly, the heavy tree shifts just enough for Shane's legs to be pulled free. Sucking in ragged breaths, I kneel by Shane's side.

"Shane! Can you hear me?" I tap his cheek urgently. "You need to get up!"

He coughs weakly, his eyes flickering open, glassy with disorientation. "Amber? What?"

"There's no time. We need to move now!" My adrenaline spiking, I pull Shane's arm over my shoulders and drag him to his feet. He cries out as weight falls on his injured leg.

Leaning heavily on me, he limps alongside, away from the encroaching flames. But we have lost precious time. The fire rages all around us now, swallowing up the forest in all directions.

I scan desperately for an escape route. The temperature is becoming unbearable, the smoke choking.

"We're trapped!" Shane rasps, with panic in his voice,

crumpling back to the ground. "Just leave me and save yourself!"

"No one gets left behind!" I help Shane up again, though my own strength is rapidly dwindling. I'm on the verge of collapse when I suddenly hear my name. Peering through the smoke, I see Mark sprinting through burning debris.

"Amber! Over here!" He waves.

In disbelief, I help Shane limp toward that beloved voice. Mark rushes to meet us, throwing Shane's other arm over his shoulder.

"Stay with me; we're getting out!" Mark says, half-dragging Shane forward.

The heat of the flames drenches my back with sweat. We push ahead slowly, the fire raging all around. My vision starts tunneling. I mentally beg my body not to fail me now. But my blood sugar is crashing after the prolonged exertion and lack of food.

"I can't ... I have to stop ..." I choke out. Mark glances over, seeing me swaying unsteadily. Other people come rushing forward, and Mark lets go of Shane so they can take him. He sweeps me up in his arms without hesitation.

"Hold on tight, I've got you now," he urges.

I cling weakly to him as he carries me while I slip in and out of consciousness. I hear shouts and force my eyes open to see others rushing to help. Mark gently lays me on a stretcher.

"You're going to be just fine," Mark tells me, clasping my hand. I manage a faint smile before my vision goes black.

* * *

As my eyes flutter open, the sterile, bright light of the hospital room greets me, blurring gradually into focus. The memory of collapsing while fighting the wildfire rushes back, and a sense of vulnerability washes over me.

I turn slightly, noticing the IV drip attached to my arm and the rhythmic beeping of the monitor behind me. I see Mark slouched in a chair with his elbows on his knees and hands buried in his hair. He looks up wearily as I stir.

"Hey," I croak, my throat raw. "What happened?"

Dr. Homes approaches. "Good to see you awake, Amber. You gave us quite a scare," the doctor begins, her voice calm and reassuring. "You experienced a severe hypoglycemic attack. Your blood sugar levels dropped dangerously low while you were out there."

The words sink in, and images of the wildfire, of me struggling, flash through my mind. Mark ... he was there. He saved me, didn't he?

"To prevent this from happening again, especially given your active role as a volunteer firefighter, it's crucial to manage your hypoglycemia proactively," Dr. Homes continues, pulling up a chair beside my bed. "First, make sure to have regular meals and snacks that are balanced in carbohydrates, protein, and fats. It's important to keep your blood sugar levels stable throughout the day."

She hands me a pamphlet, its pages filled with dietary recommendations and tips on managing hypoglycemia. I've seen it before and thought I was managing everything just fine.

The doctor continues, "Also, always carry some form of fast-acting carbohydrate with you. If you feel any symptoms starting, take them immediately."

I nod.

"Monitoring your blood sugar levels before, during, and after any strenuous activity is crucial. Adjust your meals or snacks based on your activity level to prevent your levels from dropping too low."

Dr. Homes's words make me aware that I haven't been doing the best job of taking care of myself since the fire broke out.

"And most importantly, let those around you know about your condition. It's vital they understand what to do in case you need assistance."

As she speaks, my eyes drift to Mark. I feel guilty for the fear I must have put him through by collapsing.

"Thanks," I reply, and the doctor gets up and slips out the door.

Mark's brow furrows. "I had no idea you had blood sugar issues, Amber. You never showed any signs when we hiked together."

"Yeah, I usually manage it fine," I reply slowly, foggy memories returning. "But I pushed myself too hard back there, I guess."

Mark leans forward, fear flashing across his face. "You collapsed out there, Amber! You could have died! Why didn't you tell me hypoglycemia could be a problem? Are you diabetic?"

I look away, shame welling up inside me, mixing with defiance. "No, I'm not diabetic," I reply quietly. "I've always handled it before."

Mark grabs my hand gently, waiting until I meet his eyes. "You scared the hell out of me. Please, don't keep these things from me, especially if it puts you in danger. Your health has to come first before this job or anything else."

"Hey, I'm going to be fine. This is just a minor setback. It's not like I have cancer or something awful like that."

"Thank God."

There's a commotion at the door, and I look up to see Mom and my brothers rushing toward me.

"Amber?" My mom's face is creased with worry.

"I'm fine, Mom."

Grady puts his hands on his hips. "Don't you have enough on your plate without running off into the woods to fight fires every damn day?"

"My thoughts exactly," Mark adds.

Matt comes over, crouches down, and softly whispers, "You can't single-handedly save everyone. Nor can you undo the past, kiddo. So quit trying." He pats my arm. A tear slides down my cheek. He's right.

"We all care about this town and the neighboring communities. No one is more proud of you than we are. But sometimes you've got to think about your needs, honey." Mom wipes a tear from her eye. "Maybe it's time you take a break and go someplace else for a while. Leave town." She glances over at Mark, and he nods.

"Doctor's orders," Dr. Homes says from behind my family.

I smile. "I wonder where I should go. I can't go hiking on my favorite trail anymore."

"I think we can work something out." Mark chuckles.

Chapter Nineteen

Amber

At the base of the mountain trail, I slip on my mask so I don't damage my lungs. I'm not going far. I just want to see everything for myself. Each step sends a puff of gray ash into the air. As I climb higher, I come upon the devastation. All around me are nothing but ghostly skeletons of once healthy pines, now reduced to just blackened spikes.

I shrug. I've hiked here since childhood. These mountains have always been a healing place for me. It's surreal being here now.

This trail holds so many memories—happy times with my family and friends, racing my brothers up the path, and telling ghost stories while cooking s'mores over the fire. Getting stalked by a cougar and crossing paths with a bear. And leading groups of tourists on their first hike. Holding Derek's hand as we took in the views. I let out a sigh.

I think back to the hike with Mark. I have to give Mark credit—that hike started out challenging for him. But he persevered with determination, not wanting me to think he couldn't handle it. I remember how his forehead beaded with sweat, his face set in a mixture of concentration and stubbornness as he pressed on.

I laugh as I recall the tent fiasco and our first rain-soaked night. Mark mistook my offer to share my sleeping bag as a romantic invitation. He soon learned that his usual charm wasn't going to work on me so easily.

Then I remember our last night camping, drinking wine, sitting under the vast, starry sky. That's when it hit me. I'd been developing feelings for him; feelings I hadn't thought I'd experience again. I was afraid he'd just disappear, and I didn't want to get my heart broken.

But it turned out Mark was not who I first thought he was. When signs of the forest fire appeared, he stepped up, demonstrating he was more than capable, by helping me lead other hikers to safety. And he stayed around rather than rush back to Texas. His financial support paid for supplies and places for people to stay.

When Veronica showed up and told me she slept with Mark, I was devastated. But I forgave him once he revealed his past. Telling me things he was ashamed of about himself—his difficult childhood and his blind determination to make something of himself—the people he had displaced, along with his regret. He told me about Veronica and their toxic relationship. Mark even confessed that he didn't know what love was until he met me.

The path is now a graveyard of trees. Not wanting to go any farther, I turn back and walk down the trail.

It will take years, maybe even decades, for the land to

recover, but I know nature, much like the human heart, will find a way to heal. Just like Mark and I will grow stronger together as time goes by if we both put in the effort.

* * *

"Welcome back, Amber!" Maya greets me as I walk in the door in a 1950s-style polka-dot dress with a full shirt and tight bodice. It's good to wear something other than my firefighting clothes or jeans and a T-shirt for a change.

"It's so nice to be back!" I give her a quick squeeze. "Thank you for holding down the shop."

"Oh, we managed alright," she assures me. "Though the fire drove a lot of the tourists away."

The shop door swings open again, ushering in a mother and teenage daughter. I overhear the mom saying, "Look at all the cute clothes; they're so different from back home."

I approach with my best smile. "Welcome! Feel free to browse around. We brought in lots of new boho dresses and accessories this season."

"Thanks!" The daughter's eyes light up as she scopes the racks. "Mom, look at this one!"

As I help the mother hunt for her size for an embroidered peasant blouse, I pick up on another conversation by the scarf display.

"It's just so quaint here," an older woman remarks to her companion. "And to think the forest nearby was on fire not long ago."

Her friend shakes her head. "I know that fire was threatening for a bit. It's out now. But you can still smell it in the air, though."

These people have no idea what Leavenworth has endured,

but here we are, back on our feet, as vibrant and welcoming as ever.

The shop phone rings. Seeing the familiar number, I pick up.

"Mom. I was just thinking we're overdue for a coffee date …"

"Amber. It's so good to hear your voice, sweetheart," my mom says cheerfully. "I was just thinking the same thing. Are you free this afternoon?"

I glance at the shop door as a few more tourists wander in. "Mom wants to meet me later."

Maya looks up from the register and nods. "I've got it covered," she mouths.

"Looks like I am," I tell my mom. "Want to shoot for three at our favorite bakery? I think some quality time with you and a delicious cream cheese Danish is exactly what I need."

"I agree." Mom laughs. "How are you holding up, sweetie? It seems like things in town are getting back to normal after the stress of the fire."

"I feel good," I reply, surprised to find it true. While I loved being a part of the volunteer fire crew, my shop is where I belong now. "Maya told me business dropped while I was away. But some tourists drifted in despite the smoke from the fire."

"So … meet you at three, then?"

"Sounds like a plan."

I spend the rest of the day chatting with customers. Then I tidy a few displays before grabbing my black leather shoulder bag from behind the counter.

"All right Maya, I'm off to meet my mom. You sure you're good here solo?"

She gives me a playful, exasperated look. "Of course! I'm used to running this place by myself, remember?"

I grin. "Right, what was I thinking? Well, thanks again," I call, heading out into the welcoming sunshine and summer bustle of downtown Leavenworth.

I meander down the familiar streets, nodding hellos to the other shop owners I pass. I pause to admire the overflowing window boxes that adorn the Alpine facades. The vibrant pinks, reds, and purples of the blossoms stand out against the half-timbered buildings. It's nice to slow down and appreciate the unique beauty of this little village after weeks of combatting fires in the mountain forests.

As I near the bakery, I spot my mom seated at one of the quaint iron tables outside, a pastry box and two cups set before her.

"Amber." She waves me over with a wide smile. I bend to give her a hug before plopping into the chair opposite hers.

"Oh, it smells delicious," I sigh, peering into the pastry box filled with cream cheese Danishes, apple strudels, chocolate croissants ... my mouth waters just looking at them.

"Coffee first," Mom insists, pushing one of the tall paper cups toward me.

I laugh. "You know me too well." I take a sip, savoring the rich, dark roast taste in my mouth.

Mom studies me from across the table. "It's so wonderful to have you back safe and sound. I have to say, when you first told me you were joining the volunteer fire crew this season, I'll admit I was worried. But just look at you now. You took on those fires like a warrior!"

I flush, warmed by her praise. We sit talking for another hour, nibbling pastries and basking in the normalcy of each other's company. The memory of the fire now fades away amidst our little village's bright blooms and sunshine.

Amber

Standing on the porch of my tiny cabin, I gaze out. I decide not to go for a run. The smell of smoke still permeates the mountain air, though the fire's been out for a while.

I hear the crunch of tires over the gravel drive.

"Hey there, fire girl," Mark greets me as he climbs out of the driver's seat. "Thought you could use some company today."

I make my way down the porch steps and into his waiting embrace. "You have no idea how much I was hoping you'd show up," I say, giving him a kiss.

"I promised I'd make a quick trip to the office and back."

"Will you be staying long?"

His smile turns sheepish. "Well, I'm hoping to scope out some potential properties in the area."

Of course. Mark may have fallen for small-town charm, but wheeling and dealing remains in his blood.

I hear a muffled sound coming from his car. I glance at Mark. "Did you hear that?"

His eyes glint mischievously. "Oh right, I've got a little surprise for you." He gestures to his car.

A furry brown-and-white head pops up in the passenger window, ears perked excitedly. My heart leaps as I take in those familiar soft eyes and lopsided ear. It's the abandoned pup I rescued from under the porch just days before the area went up in flames.

"What are you doing with her?" I ask Mark, confused.

Mark rubs the back of his neck. "Well, here's the thing. The shelter contacted her owners, but they made it pretty clear they didn't want the responsibility of owning a dog anymore. It turns out they were just renting the place, and while they were there, the dog ran off. They got tired of looking for her, and when the fire broke out, they returned to Idaho without her."

That poor, sweet dog was abandoned not once, but twice.

"C'mon out, girl!"

The dog lets out a volley of happy barks and throws herself through the open car window. She hits the ground running, kicking up fine ash dust in her race toward me.

"Do you remember me?" I kneel to catch her flailing paws as she tries to lick every inch of my face. Her fur still bears a slight smokey scent, though fresh baths have restored its fluffy texture. Beneath the joyful chaos, I feel her whole body quivering with excitement.

I glance up at Mark through the enthusiastic kisses and wagging tail assault. "So what does this mean? Did you find someone to take her?"

He shrugs, looking almost shy. "Well, after I heard she

didn't have a home, and I know how much rescuing her meant to you ..."

My throat tightens. "You want me to keep her?" I bury my face in her soft neck fur to hide sudden tears.

"Only if you want," Mark adds gently. "But she seems happy to see you again."

He crouches, one hand stroking the dog's back. "She's a special one. Reminds me of a certain firefighter I know." He grins, his eyes meeting mine. "So, what do you think? Do you want her?"

The dog turns her head toward me then, too. Those big, soulful eyes looking at me. My heart squeezes. It whimpers, almost like it's talking to me. Asking me not to leave it alone again.

"I know, sweetheart," I murmur into its fur. "No one's abandoning you now."

I look over at Mark. "Yes," I whisper. "Yes, I would love to keep her," saying aloud what I've held secret since I first gazed into this sweet furry face. "She can go to work with me and greet everyone who comes into my store. And when I'm gone, she can play with Bobby's dog out at Kim and Ethan's ranch."

Mark's arms encircle us both then as he plants a kiss on the dog's brow. "Then it's settled. Welcome home, girl."

"Does she have a name already?" I ask.

"They were calling her Patty at the shelter. But I figured you should have the honor of naming her yourself."

I consider this. I'm glad I rescued her. Now, she gets a second chance at life, love, and a forever home.

"Phoenix," I finally say. "I'll name her Phoenix."

Mark grins. "I think that's absolutely perfect."

I fetch several old blankets to make Phoenix a bed on the

porch. But she insists on following me inside instead, promptly curling up on my area rug.

The cozy warmth settles around me like a soft blanket as I watch Mark roam around my cabin. His presence in my space is new yet oddly comforting.

"It's starting to feel homey here," he remarks, his eyes scanning the familiar surroundings.

I lean against the counter. "Homey?" A smile teases the corners of my lips. "You mean like home?"

"Yeah." He turns to face me. "Mind if I get a beer?" he asks, already moving toward the fridge.

"Beer? I thought you were a wine connoisseur, like my brother, Chris?" I tease.

He pulls out a beer and pops the cap, leaning back against the fridge. "I like both," he says. "But I feel like a beer today."

"Oh?" I'm curious about this sudden change.

He takes a slow sip of his beer, his gaze holding mine. "It's nice not having to play the role of a wealthy business owner all the time," he confesses, a hint of weariness in his voice. "Inside, I'm just a kid from the streets of Chicago."

I move closer, my heart warming at his vulnerability. "I'm glad you came back," I admit softly.

Mark sets down his beer, his eyes sparkling. "Hey, you're going to be glad when I'm off on business," he teases with a half-smile, "because you're going to get sick of all the attention I'm giving you when I'm here."

Before I can protest, he steps forward, wrapping his arms around me. His kiss is electric, sending a jolt straight through me. My knees buckle, and I cling to him, lost in the intensity of the moment. I can't help but melt into him, forgetting everything but the feel of his lips on mine.

Epilogue

Mark

Amber insists I accompany her to her family dinner. It's part of the package of being in her life. A family gathering like this is unfamiliar territory for me, a stark contrast to eating in restaurants with people I don't know or care about.

I'm carrying a dish brimming with healthy vegetables, Amber's contribution to tonight's meal. Meanwhile, she leads Phoenix on a leash, proud to show off her new pup. As we walk around the back of her mom's B&B, I hear her siblings in a lively debate about their favorite sports teams, with bets on the outcomes of several games.

"Who's this?" Bobby, Kim and Ethan's son, runs over to greet Phoenix.

"It's my new dog," Amber tells him. "I rescued her during the fire. Her owners didn't want her, and Mark was nice enough to make sure I got to keep her."

"Can I play with her?" Bobby asks.

"Sure, go ahead." Amber hands over the leash to him, and Bobby leads the dog off around the yard, where he throws a ball for Phoenix to chase.

The aroma of BBQ chicken sizzling on the grill tantalizes my senses as we draw closer. I can't help but feel my mouth water in anticipation.

Amber's brother, Matt, is by the grill, dishing up the meat on a platter. He catches my eye and throws a casual invitation my way. "You up for some touch football after we eat?" he asks.

The truth is, I've always been competitive. Still, my experience with sports is limited to my childhood playing basketball at the park and cheering from the sidelines at the sports arena as an adult. I nod, trying to sound more confident than I am. "Sure, just don't go too hard on me," I respond with a half-smile.

I turn to find my best friend, Ethan, sauntering over. He claps a hand on my shoulder. "Glad you decided to stick around. I had a feeling you and Amber would hit it off."

I can't help but smile, thinking back to his wedding and how Ethan had slyly orchestrated the hike with Amber. My gaze drifts to where she's arranging the place settings, her dark hair catching the last rays of the sun. She's a breathtaking sight, and even now, she has the power to leave me speechless.

"She's one hell of a woman," I say, unable to take my eyes off her.

Ethan chuckles. "Glad you took my advice."

I nod, my mind briefly flickering to Veronica. "It cost me the hotel deal in Chicago. But she's worth it," I admit, feeling a sense of conviction in my words.

Ethan grins, a knowing look in his eyes. "Women can be expensive, but you made the right decision."

"Ain't that the truth?"

We share a moment of laughter, an unspoken understanding between us. As I look back at Amber, her laughter mingling with her sister Kim's in the evening air, I know that no matter what challenges lie ahead, being here with her is exactly where I belong.

As I approach the table, Amber's sister Kim recounts her honeymoon adventures. "The beaches were stunning, pure white sand against tropical blue waters," she gushes.

Grady cuts in with a smirk, "Yeah, paradise perfect, right, sis?"

Matt throws a playful jab. "Did you just barricade yourself in your bungalow, living off room service the whole time?"

Laughter dances around the table. I gently squeeze Amber's hand.

Martha chimes in with a knowing smile, "Oh, let them be. We all know what honeymoons are for."

Matt turns to Amber. "Got any travel plans coming up?"

I glance at Amber, a playful challenge in my eyes. "So, where do you plan on going?"

She looks up, surprised, holding a forkful of salad. "Going? What do you mean?"

I lean in closer. "Doctor's orders, remember?"

Amber's lips curve into a thoughtful smile. "Haven't really thought about it. You planning to be my travel buddy?"

I can't help but grin. "Absolutely. Paris, Italy, the Bahamas ... you name it, and I'll make it happen."

She is pondering the thought but then says, "How about a hiking trip in Bavaria?"

"Bavaria? Really?"

She teases. "Too challenging for you?"

I grin. "If Bavaria is what you want, then Bavaria it is."

Her eyes light up. "You'd do that for me?"

I whisper, half-joking, half-serious, "I'd charter a rocket to the moon and back if it made you happy."

Grady lets out a low whistle while Kim rolls her eyes at my comment.

Amber playfully adds, "But you'll have to leave your cell phone behind."

I feign horror. "Now that's crossing the line." But we both know I'd do it in a heartbeat.

"You're making me look bad, Mark." Grady laughs. "Jess will be searching the internet for places she'll want me to take her."

Jess smiles. "Darn right, I will."

Everyone laughs.

"Can Phoenix stay with us while you're gone?"

"You bet," I reply to Bobby while winking at Kim.

Martha passes a plate of corn on the cob. "Now that the fire is over, what are your plans, Mark?"

A spread of delicious-looking food lines the table, and I fill my plate as dishes are passed around. "Well, I'm going to look at some land on the other end of town along the river. Thought it might be nice to build a small resort geared toward outdoor enthusiasts."

"Yes, whitewater rafting trips, snow adventures, and hiking in areas that didn't burn," Amber offers with enthusiasm.

"Oh, how wonderful," Martha beams. "We could certainly use a place like that around here."

Grady leans forward. "When you're ready to move on it, let me know. Our construction company could use the project."

"Yes, I was hoping to talk to you about that."

"So, things must be serious between you two, then?" Chris asks Amber.

Amber blushes but doesn't avoid the question. "Yeah, they are. We've been through a lot together."

Her brothers groan, but their smiles give them away.

"Another Holloway bites the dust," Grady teases.

Laughing, Amber swats his shoulder, then nestles closer beside me. I slip my arm around her, relaxing into this newfound sense of family. One day, I'll look back on this place and these people as the beginning of learning what a loving home and family feel like.

Acknowledgments

I would like to thank my husband and friends for their support. Especially the ladies in my book club for not getting upset with me when I haven't read the month's book. A special thanks goes to the editors that have helped make my stories better and my cover designer for her wonderful designs.

I also want to thank the lady volunteer firefighters who helped me with getting some of the details right in this story.

My house hasn't been as tidy and my meals haven't been fancy while I've been sitting at my computer dreaming up stories. But my family understands in order to create it takes time. I am thankful for everyone's understanding.

Love you all!

Judy

Judy's been accused of having an overactive imagination since she was a child. So it only made sense that she jot down her stories and turn them into books.

She lives in the Pacific Northwest and splits her time between living in a city on the water and a cabin in the mountains of Leavenworth, Washington.

In addition to writing contemporary small town romances, Judy writes mystery romances that have strong emotional elements found in woman's fiction. Her Cook's Cove series contains a little bit of heat along with some darker themes.

For more information about Judy's books go to her website at www.judy-leslie.com

www.ingramcontent.com/pod-product-compliance
Lightning Source LLC
Chambersburg PA
CBHW072137300726
48975CB00003B/1105